MW01007933

IMPOSSIBLE

NAKED

LIFE

Impossible Naked Life
© 2022 by Luke Rolfes
All Rights Reserved
First Edition

No part of this book may be used or reproduced in any manner whatsoever without written permission except in the case of brief quotations embodied in critical articles or reviews.

Attention schools and businesses: For discounted copies and large orders please contact the publisher directly.

Kallisto Gaia Press
1801 E. 51st Street
Suite 365-246
Austin TX 78723
info@kallistogaiapress.org

Cover Art: *Muse* by Larry Crawford
          acrylic on paper (8.5" X 11.5")
Edited by Tony Burnett

ISBN: 978-1-952224-17-1

IMPOSSIBLE NAKED LIFE

STORIES

LUKE ROLFES

FOR
Valerie

TABLE OF CONTENTS

1.

2.

3.

4.

1.

Crab

SHE CLAPPED HER HANDS and said "I'm supposed to love Cancers," when she found out his birthday. Her name was Bobbi. Even though he went by Robert, she insisted they be known as the Bobbies. Her favorite restaurant was Red Lobster— imagine that. She told the hostess, "A booth for two Bobbies." He had never dated someone like her. When they returned to her apartment, she said "I can be terrible sometimes" and took off her shirt.

On their fourth date she showed up at his place with a 10-gallon aquarium. Inside: a bed of sand and rocks, and four colorful shells that moved.

"Hermit crabs," she explained. They already had names: Pinch, Claw, Battle-Crab, and Leonard.

Robert tapped on the glass. The crabs became shells. "How about Greek food?" he asked. She shook her head and took off her shirt. They did the thing he had been waiting four dates to do. Again and again. Next to the bed, the Hermit crabs skittered in their cage.

It snowed for days, and Robert and Bobbie spent nights huddled next to the space heater watching movies on her laptop. She put the aquarium next to the heater and fed the crabs lettuce and saltine crackers. Leonard, the biggest, peeked out long enough to pincer a hunk of salad before retreating under a spiral shell. Robert got used to the little creatures after a while.

Their rooting around after he turned out the lights soothed him to sleep.

On the first night of February, they had a terrible fight. Bobbie said she would no longer sleep over.

"You hate my friends and my sisters. You won't meet my mom."

"But I love you," he insisted.

"You love what we do at night."

"Is that wrong?"

"What are my sisters' names?"

"I don't remember."

"It's not that you don't remember. It's that you don't care." She plucked Claw out of the aquarium. "What is this crab's name?"

"I don't remember."

"Fine," she said. With her fingers, she tugged the tiny crustacean out of its yellow shell, stuck it in her mouth, and swallowed.

"Are you insane?"

"I gave them to you, and you don't care."

In shock, he watched her eat Pinch next, and then Battle-Crab. "I'm sorry I didn't listen," he said.

She pulled the final crab out of the aquarium. It squirmed in her hand.

"No," he said. "Not Leonard."

Day Camp

LAST JULY, MY BOYFRIENDS FAMILY took me to an RV campground outside of Moline, Illinois. The resort had a lodge with a diner in it that served delicious cornmeal pancakes, green and orange paddleboats for rent, an indoor pool, miniature golf, and all sorts of activities that might entertain people who live their lives on this property throughout the summer months.

The thing to do in these campgrounds, I realized, is sit in nice lawn chairs and wait for people to come by. Every twenty minutes, someone new would arrive to the circle of chairs. They shared gossip and cold drinks. Sometimes the visitors would bring candy or cookies. It reminded me, a bit, of being in college—how people would just pop by if you left your dorm room door ajar.

We stayed in one of the rental cabins without air conditioning. Luckily, in the late afternoon, a thunderstorm rolled through the Mississippi Valley, and that dropped the sweltering temperature by twenty degrees. My boyfriend spent the evening, post storm, drinking Miller Lites with his cousins and uncles around the campfire. I played with all of their ignored children at the rusty playground, not feeling entirely welcome at the fire—but not exactly unwelcome either. I realized at some point in the night that my boyfriend and I were going to break up soon. Not immediately, but surely in the next several months.

Early the next morning, unable to sleep with the daylight streaming through the cabin windows, I went for a jog through the campground and surrounding highways. When I returned, the only person awake was my boyfriend's niece, so I decided to walk her over to the diner to get breakfast.

My boyfriend's grandfather, a heavy man with speckled skin, was already sitting at a booth and drinking coffee. I remembered then that this was his campground—the place he lived six months of the year—and that he was the person who had invited us out. He waved me and his great granddaughter over.

"You're the only guy in this crew who doesn't sleep in," I said.

"I've been awake for hours," he said. "Always been an early bird. I like to sit in here and watch everybody get up. I seen you out running at 6:15. You were gone about 35 minutes."

He ordered me and his great granddaughter cornmeal pancakes, which turned out to be the best I've ever had. In the moment, I didn't comprehend that he was the first male in my boyfriend's family to acknowledge me, but I did have a sudden realization about what it was like to be older. Not so much an awareness of choices and time passed, but more so an understanding of where you are in the universe and when individuals are moving in and out of your orbit. Something about this grandfather's smile and posture seemed to illustrate this idea. His life was almost over. I don't know if he knew that or not. He died later that year just before my boyfriend and I split for good. But he seemed in the diner—the only time I ever talked to him—to understand that I was a one-time visitor in this land, and that I didn't belong there.

The Birds of Joy

DOWN THE HALL OF SCREAMS the men in plastic suits go by with another body in a wheelbarrow. The fifth one today—a woman in her mid-sixties. Dr. Tahim is seated in a folding chair, eating a ham sandwich with one hand and signing a notepad the nurse is sticking in his face with the other. He hasn't eaten for a long time. He can't remember when he last shaved or showered. Earlier, when he looked in the dirty bathroom mirror, the gray in his cheeks surprised him.

"How about a bite," says the nurse. Tahim holds up the sandwich and the nurse nips a hunk off the corner. Part of the ham slides out of the bread and dangles from her lips. With her middle finger, she pushes the ham inside her mouth. "This is my joy," the nurse says, and then leaves.

The lights in the hall of screams flicker. A voice yelling in a foreign language. The sound of rubber boots squeaking on the tile.

Another nurse comes by, a young Latino. He sits on Tahim's lap. There is nowhere else to sit.

"It feels good to sit," says the nurse. "Sitting is my joy."

"My pants have blood on them," says Tahim. "You should be on the other side."

The nurse moves to his opposite leg. Tahim curls his arm

around the nurse's neck and takes another bite of sandwich.

"Did you hear about the birds?" the nurse asks.

"Are they carriers now?"

The nurse shakes his head. "Samantha—you know how she gets—overrode the automatic doors. The heat was melting the equipment, she claimed, so she took matters into her own hands. One of the med students found her later in the break room. She had stripped off her shirt and was sitting on top of the table drinking two cups of coffee at once. Her tits were covered in espresso and milk."

"I'll write a prescription," says Tahim. "Something to help her sleep."

The nurse continues. "Everybody laughed when the first bird flew in. 'Get a couple brooms and a sheet,' a man from the waiting room yelled. But then the birds kept coming. Two, then four. Then a continuous wave. Hundreds, could be thousands, streaming in through the automatic door. Finally, Edward manually pulled the entrance closed. Outside, on the sidewalk, became a pile of stunned birds. All following the tail-feathers in front of them. Ramming the glass at full speed."

"My leg is asleep," says Tahim.

The nurse sighs and stands. He holds out his pad and Tahim scribbles a signature. The nurse flips the page and Tahim signs. The nurse flips the page again, and Tahim signs again.

"Try not to worry," he tells the nurse. "The birds will eventually find their way out. My joy is being free from worry."

He stands, as well, rubs his beard and stretches. He and the nurse walk in opposite directions down the corridor—the doctor toward the hall of screams, the nurse away.

Before starting his afternoon rounds, Tahim decides to visit Mrs. Anderson, the woman in the corner room with two windows. Her doorway is wide, and he can hear the mounted television playing the monotonous babble of the news channel.

"How is your breathing this afternoon, Mrs. Anderson?" he says when he walks into her room. The old lady, in her 80's, is sitting up and drinking a glass of ice water through a paper straw.

"I want to be put on a ventilator," she says.

"You don't need it."

"I talked to my daughter this morning. She says it's important to reserve my ventilator right away."

"We have plenty of ventilators."

"Let me borrow your pen, doctor. I'll write my name on one."

"Please lean forward, Mrs. Anderson. I'm going to listen to your lungs now."

The elderly woman does as told. Dr. Tahim presses his stethoscope on her bony back. Through the earbuds, her old heart clangs; her lungs fill and un-fill.

"Your breathing sounds beautiful, Mrs. Anderson. You've been blessed."

The lights dim and flicker again. The sound of yelling farther down the hall of screams. A tall man in a plastic suit runs past the doorway, boots squeaking.

"You said you would talk to them about putting sheets in the wheelbarrows," Mrs. Anderson says.

"Next time. I promise," he says. He smiles and pats her arm. "Now, as soon as you tell me your joy, I will continue my rounds and you can resume your television program."

Mrs. Anderson thinks for a moment and then says, "Joy came to me this morning."

She pulls away the blanket next to her. Underneath is a metal bedpan, inside of which sits a tiny starling—shaking its head and blinking in the sudden light. The bird scans the room, looking at the doctor, and then Mrs. Anderson, and then back to the doctor. It stands briefly on twig legs, but then ruffles its feathers and settles into the bedpan, uninterested in flight.

Paperboy

A PAPERBOY DISAPPEARED from the streets of Des Moines, Iowa when I was a baby. News of his absence rang through the state for years. If you see a kid slinging a massive tote filled with cellophane-wrapped shoppers and registers, you know his mom and dad had with him the talk about vanishing paperboys. All of us sat through "the talk." Don't look at the old man who offers you corn muffins and the warmth of a kerosene heater. Don't let the woman who sleeps underneath the band shell in Lyons Park touch your face, even though she says it will heal her. Hold out your hand to dogs, fingers down, especially the ones without collars and ears that pull flat alongside their thick necks. Above all else: Don't, under any circumstance, disappear.

Every day—sometime between night and dawn—I completed my route. I never broke any of the rules in my time as a paperboy, though I did see once a naked man and woman pressed against their living room windows. The couple had their limbs spread like one of those suction-cup-Garfield-cats you used to see on car windows—or like the man and the woman were specimens caught between microscope slides and cover slips. Dark hair grew across the man's pale skin, thickest in the patches between his nipples and hips. Flattened against the window, the woman's heavy breasts and abdomen were covered in purple stretch marks that I thought at the time were scratches and welts. The naked couple stared at me as I stepped across the walkway and set their paper on the front porch. When I looked back the

9

man had moved behind the woman, and they seemed to be just standing there, hugging each other as the sun rose across the neighborhood.

And then there was the other time when that young girl with the ratted hair came out of the woods holding a giant bull snake. The fat, checkered snake, five or six feet long, had its tail wrapped around her right arm. She had the back of its head gripped with her left, and the snake extended its slender snout in slow circles, trying to find a place to land its teeth.

"Pick a house," the girl said. She was barefoot with socks of dirt. It took me a moment to realize she was talking to me.

"Pick a house, paperboy," she said again. "The whole city is unlocked."

I shifted my tote on my shoulder and pointed to a split foyer across the cul-de-sac. The people who lived in that house never paid their bill.

The girl walked toward the property I had fingered, stroking the snake whose bottom half was now circling her neck. When she reached the edge of the streetlights, I lost track of her in the darkness. I wasn't sure what was next, so I continued to trek down my route, tossing cellophane packages on stoops or slipping them into the creak of mail slots.

I had a thought at the end of the street that has stuck with me to this day. From where I stood, in the middle of Iowa, fast moving rivers surrounded me. Rivers on both sides of the state, and a river splitting the city to the north and south. The snakes, the naked couple, the disappeared paperboys. We all lived somewhere in between these rivers, cut off in every direction.

You are not Listening

CAMILA IS RIDING HER HOVERBOARD in the cul-de-sac. She has beautiful, long hair and olive skin. She and Matthew are in the same grade, but she has three older sisters, so she knows more about the world than he does.

"Don't freaking touch me, Matty," she says. "Six feet."

"I wouldn't," says Matthew.

The two ride in figure eights through the cul-de-sac—Camila on her hoverboard and Matthew on his scooter. Their wheels drone on concrete as they fall into a pattern, matching each other's speed. One on the loop, one on the criss-cross. After a while, Camila says, "Yesterday, I saw a snapping turtle by the bike trail."

"Was it alive?"

"Of course it was alive. Did you know they bite and never let go? It happened to my uncle once. The turtle was stuck to his arm for hours. My dad had to cut the turtle's head off with a saw."

"Like a chainsaw?"

"Just a saw-saw. He had to do it. Nothing else could be done."

"Did your dad bury the turtle?"

"I don't think so."

"What did he do with its body?"

"Threw it in the woods, probably. Maybe just put it in a garbage can."

"What about its head?"

"Jesus, Matty. That's a stupid question if I've ever heard

11

one."

Camila breaks the looping pattern and rolls in a straight line, away from her driveway where sits on cinderblocks her dad's Thunderbird restoration project. Matthew follows her down the hill, past the blue and red playground equipment and the community fishing pond surrounded by shatter-cane and cattails. There are no other kids outside. The houses are silent, the grass still that awful shade of light yellow. The March air feels like it is trying for rain.

"Hey, there's Dean and Gene," says Matthew. "They live right behind me."

Next to the trail entrance, two older men sit on a park bench. They are holding hands and staring off into the distance of the afternoon. Matthew's parents say he needs to be extra careful not to spread germs to those two. Gene had cancer once. He almost died, but then he got better. Dean, though he doesn't have cancer, has something else. Matthew can't remember what it is.

"You kids look like you are on a mission," says Gene, the older man on the left.

"Snapping turtles, I guess," says Matthew.

The man on the right, Dean, smiles. He never says much. Gene says, "A dangerous foe. Perhaps you'll need a long net."

Camila and Matthew snoop around the bike trail entrance. They check the tall grass and edge of the stream, but there are no turtles. Still not technically spring, most of the wildlife is in hiding. A few nightcrawlers squirm after Camila rolls over a log. A handful of early water bugs dot the cold water. Neither kid ventures deeply into the surrounding forest. When Matthew looks into the trees, he thinks about a turtle shell half-buried in dirt and weeds—arms, legs, and tail accounted for but neck ending in nothingness. He doesn't know why, but he shivers.

"Any luck?" Gene asks after a while.

"None," says Matthew.

"You kids staying safe?"

Matthew nods and says "Yes, sir," but Camila doesn't say anything. The two mount their scooter and hoverboard and begin the trek up the hill. The old men on the park bench wave to them as they leave. Matthew waves back.

Camila yells down, "You're the ones who should worry about staying safe, boomer."

As they ride back up the neighborhood hill, Matthew stares as her. At the top, he says, "I don't know why you said that."

She shrugs and says, "I say that stuff to everybody."

And then she cuts in front of him on her hover board. Her long hair is an auburn waterfall cascading down her back, her clear laugh like a bell. Above his friend, Matthew notices that the houses in the neighborhood all have gray or charcoal colored roofs. And the clouds above them are also gray.

Plucked

PEOPLE AT RAILROAD CROSSINGS stare at our Amtrak train when we blast by. Kids usually wave, but adults stand there slack-jawed.

Inside the train, sleep and strangeness are currency.

The first time passengers woke me up last night: I slid off my seat when a loud voice said, Get down there, girl, and then this guy slapped his girlfriend on the ass as they descended the stairs to the disgusting-bathroom-level of the train.

The second time passengers woke me up last night: An older woman in the seat behind me tapped my shoulder until I opened my eyes. I can no longer fly, she said when I asked her what was wrong. In the air, her inner ear goes haywire for whatever reason—so much so that the ENT doctor thought her eardrums might burst at 30,000 feet. She asked me to close my eyes and imagine an old lady's body crashing back and forth between a plane's tin walls, the inside of an old lady's brains a tilt-o-whirl. Imagine the panic onboard as people hold their hands up to push away a suddenly spinning, white-haired ballerina.

The third time passengers woke me up last night: Some asshole set his phone alarm for 4:30AM.

Now, it's after dawn. Sunlight is streaming through the windows. Our train is chugging across America, and the old lady with the ear problem is snoring against the back of my seat.

The Asian man sprawled across the row next to me rises and rubs his face. He's been riding beside me since Los Angeles.

He looks over to me and says, I think I'll have my morning Budweiser.

* * *

Out the observation car windows, hazy Midwestern farmland rolls by on loop. Four senior citizen men sit at the booth behind where I work on my laptop. They are discussing, over morning coffee, the United States Women's National Soccer Team, who have recently advanced to the semi-finals of the Women's World Cup. I read on my phone yesterday that one of the American players went viral when she answered a reporter's question by saying, I'm not going to the fucking White House.

I have my back to the four seniors, so I can't tell who is talking, but I learn from their conversation that:
1. Society has a hard time identifying with the soccer team, except for the blonde who plays in the middle and seems like a real down-to-earth person.
2. Someone named Frank believes lesbianism is beautiful.
3. No one can be certain how many lesbians are on the squad, but for sure the goalie and the forward with purple hair who scores all the goals.
4. Sportsmanship isn't what it used to be.
5. Frank's brain is located inside of his penis.

I put in my ear buds and raise the volume on my work-playlist. I've been trying to finish my comparative literature thesis for about six months now, and I simply can't. It could be I'm too easily distracted. Or perhaps I'm not smart enough. All the other students in my cohort, when they talk about post-structuralism, post-colonialism, deconstructionism, liminal spaces, or what have you, talk in a discourse that is above my head. Quietly, I Google the words they use in class and pretend to know what they are talking about, but I don't have the vocabulary. I understand texts. I can talk about what they mean to me and how they reflect upon the world around me, but I simply

15

don't know how to quip and banter like the other students do.

My parents, sensing the stress of my thesis committee's deadline, paid for me to take the train home to Baltimore for my cousin Rachel's wedding. It's a three-day trip, they told me. You will be trapped in your seat, and all there is to do is work. Plus, they added, you are a basket case when you fly.

I concentrate on my thesis for as long as humanly possible, which is thirteen minutes. The seniors at the booth behind me leave and are replaced by Budweiser Guy, carrying a tallboy and a croissant. I swivel to ask him about the price of breakfast. He grunts and says, A lot more than what this shit is worth.

I'm about to get up and wander, but when I turn around I'm not alone. A dark-haired woman in her early forties—maybe fifteen or so years older than me—is sitting on the other side of my booth.

I'm not lost, she says.

Not knowing what to say, I stare at her until she keeps talking.

I needed a break.

A break? I say.

Everybody on here is so strange. And you don't seem strange. Please don't say anything weird to ruin this. Sit with me. Work on your laptop, and let's not say anything at all.

Alright, I say.

I didn't sleep last night, she continues. There's no way a person can sleep surrounded by so many whackos. I paid for a sleeper car tonight, though. It was an extra two hundred dollars, but I don't care. The people in my room are leaving. I can go in there as soon as we hit Chicago.

How far is Chicago?

We passed Kansas City this morning. I think it's six or seven hours from there.

How long have you been on the train?

Since Flagstaff.

I've been on since California.

No more talking, she says. Go back to work.

I'm not sure what to do, so I bend my neck toward the

screen and try to concentrate. After a few minutes of reading and re-reading the same paragraph, my eyes drift up to meet the woman's. She smiles and points at my laptop.

Work, she says. Talk later.

I take a long breath. And then I start pecking away at chapter four, which has something to do with the poetry of Emily Dickinson in comparison to the lyrics of Madonna's Like a Prayer album. I have no idea what I'm talking about, but, for some reason or another, the words begin to flow through my fingers. With her hands folded on the tabletop, the dark-haired stranger stares out the window at the passing landscape. I can sense she is there, but, at the same time, I am all-at-once engrossed in the words I'm typing.

* * *

When I check the clock, over two hours have passed. I've written almost three thousand words.

Oh my God, I say aloud, but the other side of the booth is empty. The dark-haired stranger is gone. So is Budweiser Guy. So are the seniors talking about the United States Women's National Soccer Team. There are several new people in the viewing car. Some kids playing iPads. A man and wife who are Amish or Mennonite or something. A train custodian cleaning the glass in front of a few people sleeping in the sunlight like housecats.

I brought you a turkey sandwich, says a voice to my left.

I thought you were gone.

No, not gone. Hungry, the dark-haired woman says and sets a wax-paper package in front of me.

Wow, thank you. Let me give you some money.

No money. Eat.

Having not had breakfast or lunch, I open the sandwich and dig in. The turkey is dry but doesn't taste so bad. I say, "Didn't you bring something to do on the train? It's such a long haul."

My life is terribly busy. Usually when I get a free minute I meditate, she says. Looking out the window is fine. I get by with that.

The middle of the country, I say and gesture to the passing landscape. It's a wasteland. I've never been so bored.

I'm not bored. But I had an idea in my head that taking the train would be more exciting. Less… provincial.

The dry sandwich sticks to my throat. I wish I had something to wash it down. As if on cue, the woman reaches into her tote bag and produces two bottles of Diet Dr. Pepper. I don't drink soda anymore, but I can't refuse.

I crack the bottle and say, You're Lucy.

She says, "And you know that's my name because you see it written on my bag."

"That's right."

"I could have written a fake name on the bag. Or I could have stolen it."

"But I don't think you did."

"You can never be sure about people."

I smile, in spite of myself. The woman—Lucy—seems fun, interesting at the least. I wish she were ten years younger, or maybe that I was a ten years older.

We talk and sip soda. Maybe forty-five minutes. Maybe an hour and a half. About everything and nothing. I learn that we are both going to weddings in the Baltimore area (not the same one) and that she's a first-grade teacher. Like me, she's never ridden Amtrak. She doesn't talk about whether or not she is married, or has children, or anything about a significant other. I know it's impolite to ask. There is no ring on her finger, though, and I get the sense from the way she talks that she is recently divorced or separated.

One thing is for certain, she says. I'm done sleeping next to strangers. Never again.

Nodding, I say, "Personal space doesn't exist on a train."

"It's like we're in their bedroom," she says. "Or they are in ours."

"I get that."

"And they don't mind touching you."

"They sure don't," I say. "Totally inappropriate."

18

"Or massaging your feet while you sleep. They don't think that's off limits. And they act like you are the strange one for threatening to scream."

* * *

There's something special about arriving in Chicago. One evening, when I was a kid, my parents and I flew a lap around the city because the runway was full at O'Hare. My young eyes couldn't get over the view of the lit skyscrapers huddled alongside the endless stretch of lake. Twenty years later, as our train creeps into the metro, the oncoming skyline still entrances me.

One of the conductors walks by and raps the table with his knuckles. "Afternoon, folks," he says.

"Good afternoon," Lucy says.

The conductor begins to tell us about a severe thunderstorm chasing our train across the Midwest and how we shouldn't wander too far from the station during the layover. But I am not listening because I hear people in the booth next to us giggling. Out the window, there is a group of teenage girls gathered on the corner. They are wearing what looks to be cardboard boxes.

At first, I don't realize what I'm staring at, but then it dawns on me that the girls are pretending to be robots. There is an old boom-box stereo in front of them. The girls have drawn ridiculous dials and sensors on the cardboard. Some are wearing boxes on their heads with faces and antennae. They are doing the robot dance and waving at cars.

I can't help it. I start to laugh.

Lucy presses her face against the glass. The robot girls are shrinking in the distance, but I know she can see them when her eyes light up and she grins into the window. She pulls back, happy.

A small circle of fog remains on the glass from where her nose and mouth had been. I pretend to look out the window, but, really, I'm watching the small ring of fog as it disappears.

* * *

When the train comes to a slow, hissing halt in Union Station, Lucy leaves—likely off to scope out her private sleeper car. She doesn't say goodbye. Instead, she says, I'll talk to you at some point tonight. Then she rises and exits the viewing room. Not sure what to do next, I hike back to my seat, two cars back. Budweiser Guy is parked there, picking his teeth with a toothpick.

"Hey, man," he says. "Let's go get a fucking deep dish."

Fifteen minutes later, Budweiser Guy and I detrain and tramp through Chicago streets. Gray clouds fill the air above the skyline. He has his phone out with Google Maps open, and he's directing us toward a place with swear-to-God-three-inch-thick crust.

Without a sense of where Lake Michigan is, I'm completely lost in the cityscape of faceless people, cars, and high-rises. I don't have a reason to mistrust Budweiser Guy, though it seems a little reckless to follow a stranger into the heart of a major city.

"Do you feel that?" he yells over his shoulder.

"Yeah, the wind picked up," I say.

"Right. And the temp dropped. Big time. We're about to get shit on."

Eventually, we find the pizza joint. It's half full of patrons and dimly lit by tube lights under green shades. We find a seat at a high top. Budweiser Guy orders us a pitcher-of-guess-what and says that I have to watch him do his act—it's so hilarious— where he strikes up conversations with regulars seated at the bar about what would happen if Michael Jordan played a game of PIG against Steph Curry.

"You're from the West Coast," he says. "So you can recognize a pure shooter when you see one. These Chi-town idiots will defend Mike to the death. You have to watch. Watch how mad they get. It's so funny."

Later, after splitting a deep dish and irritating a good portion of the clientele, Budweiser Guy is in a great, giggly mood.

20

He and I jog back to Union Station through the sound of steady, rumbling thunder and cloud-to-cloud lightning. The sky is legitimately dark now, and intermittent drops of rain strike my face, shirt, and arms. No pedestrians are out, and traffic has all but disappeared, which is odd for a city the size of Chicago. It seems that everybody is inside bracing for the severe thunderstorm that seems to be inching closer and closer.

I think about Lucy as I run through the city. I wonder if she found her room on the train, and if she is looking out the window. Waiting for the storm to arrive.

* * *

Back aboard Amtrak, Budweiser Guy leaves to, as he says, zone the fuck out and watch two hours of Youtube on his phone, so I take my laptop back to the viewing car. I figure I can take in the storm through the large windows, and maybe work for two or three more hours.

A vibrant crowd has formed in the lounge area. The train feels chillier. We've picked up a number of passengers in the Chicago terminal, and the booths are full. There is an open seat, though, in a string of chairs facing the window. I snag it before anyone else decides to switch.

I open my thesis, determined to get back in the zone but immediately wish for Wifi or someone to talk to. Somewhere between Lucy and deep-dish pizza, my motivation disappeared.

Here's my fear (or maybe the truth): An exploration of Emily Dickinson and the women of 80's pop music is a silly comparative exercise. More amusement than academic. Madonna's mother died of breast cancer. Dickinson's childhood friend died of typhus. So what? My thesis committee will be embarrassed by this document.

The train is moving again, pulling away from Union Station. Soon, we'll creep out of the metro and into the suburbs, and, maybe thirty minutes later, back into the countryside of the

American Midwest.

Closing my laptop, I stand and place my forehead against the window. I can almost feel the rain hitting me in the face. The glass is smooth and cold. I close my eyes and let my mind drift into the overcast world. What am I even doing here? This entire trip is a waste of time. I don't need to go to Rachel's wedding any more than I need to be locked inside a train car to finish my thesis. Why can't I do the things I'm supposed to do? Why can't I be smarter, or more self-assured, or more focused, or happier?

For some reason, I think about those teenagers dressed as ridiculous cardboard robots, dancing and waving to strangers for kicks. It wasn't that long ago when I was young and carefree, and everything, no matter how bizarre, seemed like something worth experiencing. I can already feel myself getting shoehorned into a certain type of life.

A hand touches my arm. I open my eyes and turn to look Lucy right in the face.

Not knowing what else to say, I motion to the window and say, "It's raining."

"I know," she says. "I can't fall asleep."

What happens next is like a dream, I guess, or an involuntary reflex. I float with Lucy through three different cars. She's leading me by the hand. I can't let go. She's what—at least ten or fifteen years older than me—but I don't care. Her long, dark hair swishes before me. A small waist but wide hips. I'm not recalling what her face looks like or what we talked about in the few hours before. Then I remember her thin lips. Green, close-set eyes. Her smirky smile. The fog on the train window.

We find her roomette, and she slides open the door. The interior is tiny. There's a pulldown bunk above, and a skinny cot below. The bed is two-thirds the width of a twin bed, and our bodies come together on top of it.

We're kissing at first, and everything is wonderful. I don't care what I look like, or that I haven't showered in two days. In the roomette, the scent of Lucy's lavender perfume, or body lotion or something overpowers the blue disinfectant smell that permeates the rest of the train.

22

Outside, the storm pounds against the window, and I struggle to regain my bearings. The last person I slept with was a friend from my undergraduate program. I was head over heels for this friend, but she wanted another guy named Anthony. She always managed to work his name into the conversation. Even right after we shared an intimate moment. Anthony's out of town again, backpacking in the Rocky Mountains. Anthony's folk band is playing at a children's hospital. Isn't that interesting?

When I was accepted into two master's programs and this girl didn't get into any, I asked her to come with me anyway. Nothing was stopping her from writing and taking more classes, and there was always next year's application. I don't know if I expected her to say yes, but I'm not sure I got over the way she said no. She told me it stung each time we made love. That was her body's way of showing that I wasn't right for her. And then she stopped answering my calls. She deleted all my texts.

Lucy's body is different. Older certainly than my friend from college, but denser and, in a way, sexier. I feel her breathing deepen. She isn't kissing with as much insistency, and after a few minutes, our mouths are no longer touching. She strokes my face, her back to the window and rain.

After a while, she says, "I'm too tired to keep going."

"We can do whatever you want to do," I say.

"Sleep. I want to fall asleep."

"Don't let me stop you," I say, and when I say it she grins and closes her eyes.

* * *

I'm not sure how long I lie next to this person on the train. Time has never felt more irrelevant. I'm barely awake, watching her sleep and running my fingers through her long, dark hair. The soft glow from headlights and faraway streetlights drift past in the night. The flicker of lightning and the steady cadence of rain on top of rain make the world seem calmer than before. Every now and then I hear people outside the roomette talking in muted voices, but other than these passing sounds, this tiny, tucked-away place seems singularly ours. It doesn't matter if everything outside the roomette is wrong. In here, things seem okay.

My eyelids feel heavy, and I know I'm close to drifting off.

"Lucy, are you sad?" I say.

She doesn't answer. I'm convinced she's already dreaming. But then she opens her eyes and looks at me.

"You and I are both sad," she says.

"Why do we feel this way?"

"We took the train to be alone. But we don't like to be alone."

"Are you happier now that I'm here?"

She closes her eyes and says, "I'd be happier if we were sleeping."

"Maybe I should go then, so you can sleep."

She pulls me closer to her, gets right up next to my ear and says, "If you try to leave I'll strangle you." And then she's giggling again. Kissing me and petting my face. She's tired. I'm tired. We can't make sense of whether or not this is us or if this is the train pushing the buttons that turn us on and make us go.

Fish Heart

NIKKI, WHO SHOULD HAVE DIED a long time ago when Spring Breaking in the Virgin Islands with her girlfriends, tells people she had her heart replaced with a pufferfish. This isn't true at all, but she did have a heart attack on the beach at Coki Point.

A St. Thomas boy had given her a drug laced with something or other that caused her heart to stop for more than a minute.

An off-duty doctor, a resident islander with dark-skin and dry-hands, had a defibrillator in her truck, and she came sprinting toward the sound of beachgoers screaming. The scene played out almost like in the movies, except that when the tense music crescendoed and Nikki's eyes burst open—not dead after all!—she was surrounded by strangers and topless (her swimsuit had been ripped down by the doctor). And then, when she tried to speak, to say something grateful or clarifying in the haze, she burped loudly and vomited daiquiris all over herself and the woman who had saved her life.

No, the heart attack didn't kill Nikki on the beach, though the electricity from the defibrillator burned her right breast and the flesh between her left ribs. She lived on—the damaged heart replaced with a spiny pufferfish that lives inside her chest, slowly beating its translucent flippers and swimming in place amongst the rest of her internal organs.

Fast forward through the next six years. Nikki graduates from college and takes a job in Denver as a marketing coordinator for a company that manufactures high-end carabineers and other various mountaineering equipment for the serious alpine and rock climbers of the world. Nikki swears off alcohol (except for special occasions) and any kind of drug from strangers. She sweats on the elliptical machine five days a week. Her coworkers invite her out on hikes, and then harder hikes, and then technical climbs, and then Nikki, herself, summits twenty-two of Colorado's fifty-three 14,000 foot peaks in less than twenty-four months.

Reaching the top of the world, like anything else, can become an obsession.

One of her co-workers, when Nikki crawls inch-by-inch to the crest of the boulder tower that marks the summit of Sunlight Peak (widely considered the third most difficult climb in Colorado), touches her arm. When she turns to look, she finds the strangest expression on the co-worker's boyish face. They are both lying stomach-down, clinging to the rock—neither one very good at bouldering. He says in a breathless voice that he is hopelessly in love with her and has been for some time. She listens to everything he has to say, and they kiss there on the summit block of Sunlight Peak because what else is she supposed to do?

They are the only ones on the mountain. She licks his lips and he tries to palm her breast through her stiff jacket—his fingers millimeters from the snout of her pufferfish heart. The co-worker's mouth tastes like Powerade and peanut butter Clif bars, and she never says anything about loving him back. Because she doesn't. She isn't sure she loves anybody in that way, or if loving another person feels anything but artificial.

What feels real though is standing for a moment on weak legs at the top of each peak. Realness is taking in the endless panorama around her and breathing thin air. It's real when the pufferfish within her ribs fills and collapses, and re-fills and collapses again.

Her fish never causes her any pain or numbness, nor does he ever fail her. He is, without question, the best heart she;s ever had.

SIREN

A TORNADO WARNING has been issued for our county. I see the alert on my phone before I recognize the dim sound in the distance—the chipped, yellow siren wailing on the corner of Running Horse Road. I'm pushing against my sleeping husband. He is groggy for a few heartbeats.

"Look," I say, holding the screen in front of his face.

"I'm not reading anymore," he says.

"No, Mark. We need to go to the basement."

And now he is wide awake, pushing aside the sheets and stumbling toward our daughter's bedroom. He doesn't look at me, or say anything to me on his way out.

Minutes later, we are pressed together in the downstairs storage closet. Our white cat is huddled between the legs of our four-year-old child. The gray cat is nowhere to be found, and my daughter is crying.

In between sobs, my daughter whispers that the tornado is going to suck up Monica. I stroke her long hair and tell her that Monica is going to be fine. The gray cat is a terrific hider, and she is likely tucked away under a bed upstairs, in between boxes of photographs and my old drawings.

My husband is also crying. Seven or eight years ago, his parents died from injuries sustained by the infamous EF-5 Joplin tornado. We were never told the specifics of their passing, but the emergency response crew explained that their two-story house had simply collapsed on itself. Like a star, my husband says when he mentions it to close friends and family members. I don't know

27

why he thinks of their loss like this—perhaps because he teaches eighth grade science—but he rationalizes their death in this way, how a star goes supernova after imploding on itself. The resulting shockwave being his parents' souls flowing into the heavens.

But Mark's tears aren't about the gray cat, nor the sound of the tornado siren penetrating the basement wall that reminds us all of his parents' house collapsing like a star. He's crying because this afternoon he scrolled through my phone while I was in the shower and found a long string of messages I had sent and received to someone else. This string of messages spun him to the worst possible conclusion.

I'm not a cheater, but I do believe you can have feelings for two people at the same time. I don't think that makes me a terrible person. "No lines were crossed," I told my husband in the bedroom, my hair dripping, my body wearing only a towel. "It's just a phase. I'm getting older. I wanted to feel young again."

He wouldn't look at me.

"Please say something," I said.

There was such sadness in his voice when he said, "I knew. I knew you would do this."

I shook my head. Tried my best to hug him, but he seemed all at once impossible to wrap my arms around.

Down in the basement, my daughter wails, her voice matching the siren on Running Horse Road. She calls again for Monica and clutches the white cat against her sunken chest. I reach for her hand, but my husband has me by the sleeve. He pulls me toward him until my mouth almost kisses his. This is the first time he's touched me all day.

"I can't go," he says. "You have to do it."

I know what he means. It's written across his face. Open the closet door. Go upstairs. Come back with the other cat or don't come back.

Killer Saltwater Crocodile Killer

IT WASN'T UNTIL LITTLE BRANDON HOL-LINSWORTH, who wasn't so little, was eaten that people started to take things seriously. It was a fine town. Isolated, as small towns tend to be, but one that had all it needed. An 18-hole championship-level golf course. A pizza place, a Mexican joint called "La Bonita," a fine-dining restaurant with a tiki bar on the water's edge, one other bar and a grocer, a hardware, a town square, and a Casey's gas station that also served pizza. There was a community hospital fifteen miles away in a town called Guthrie Center. The lake patrol transported Little Brandon Hollinsworth's upper body (which wasn't so little) to the hospital, wrapped in a clean tarp in the back of the maintenance truck. At triage, the attending physician officially pronounced the young Hollinsworth dead by saying "don't you ever bring half a corpse to my ER again," and the town, fifteen miles to the west, seemed to hear the doctor's words—the gravity of them—even though he spoke in a quiet voice, and there wasn't more than a handful of people in the waiting room.

Recognition and reaction. A wet rag pulled through the dust of people's fears. The beach, closed. Pontoon boats and kayaks, beached. Docks and jetties, roped. Adirondack chairs, garaged. Several families' floating trampoline islands, deflated. The championship-level golf course considered canceling the father-daughter weekend scramble but then had it anyway.
What could have eaten Little Brandon Hollinsworth? People

29

wanted to know. He wasn't so little. What kind of animal could have done that? Did a mountain lion maul him and stash his remains in the lake? A wayward black bear? Starving coyotes? A pack of wild dogs?

*

Mary Jo Ford, out on her morning run, was the first to see a creature she described as a saltwater crocodile, half-sunk off Christmas Tree Point.

"Not sunk," she said. "Submerged. Hiding."

Also, an important distinction, it wasn't an alligator. She was smart enough to know the difference. Its toothy, crooked face gave it away.

Backwards, she jogged up the hill toward the swimming pool and driving range, her smart phone held in front of her like a shield between jogger and beast. The American crocodile images on Google didn't look right. And even though other croc pics were closer, she was convinced the facial structure fit the build of a saltwater crocodile. There was something prehistoric about that jaw. Plus, it was big. Like big, big. It reminded her of her Uncle Todd, who had wide cheeks and sharp teeth, and always appeared to be smiling. He was also big, and he too lived by the ocean.

Carol, who worked in the animal control building, wrote "Big Todd" on the Dangerous-Creature-At-Large form. She hadn't filled out this bright yellow document in years. She checked "other" for species, and then crossed out "other" and wrote "reptile / potential crocodile." Mary Jo Ford scrolled through the zoomed-in photos she took with her phone. Carol agreed that it did sort of look like a crocodile.

"Someone probably flushed it down the toilet when it was a baby," Carol said. "I've heard of rich people keeping exotic pets." Then she asked Mary Jo Ford where she got her running outfit. It was from the Under Armour Outlet in Kansas City.

"Gear like that, how much would it cost? The whole get-up?" Carol asked. She was fiddling with the radio, rolling it back and forth between her palms as if about to make a call.

"It was a blow-out sale. Everything marked down," said Mary Joe Ford. "Pants were forty. Top was thirty, I think."

"And you can wear that stuff whenever. It's all versatile and breathable?"

Mary Jo Ford nodded, looking at the radio expectantly.

"Reynolds, come back," Carol pushed the button and said.

Seconds later, the radio spit to life. "Yeah, Boss."

"Meet me at hole 6 tee-box in fifteen, would ya? Bring your snake pole."

* * *

News of Big Todd—the prime suspect in the death of little Brandon Hollinsworth (who wasn't so little)—spread through town. People questioned how a crocodile could exist in this latitude on this continent. Some estimated that since the lake was attached to a river, that river was attached to another river, and the river that that river attached to emptied into the Gulf of Mexico, surely Big Todd could have swum up all those rivers and ended up here, in town, sunning himself by hole 6 and looking for more people to devour. Anything was possible.

To many, though, a saltwater crocodile sounded about as plausible as the Loch Ness Monster. Mary Joe Ford wasn't the most reliable source in the universe. She was pretty and airy like pâte à choux, said the town baker who always used food metaphors, but there wasn't a lot to her of sustenance. The town baker had seen the croc pics on Facebook, and he thought they looked photoshopped. Two years ago, he and Mary Joe Ford had gone on two dates, and they had ended badly—kissing in her apartment like they were falling in love, and then going nowhere. She was present one second, living in the moment. The next she was buttoning her shirt and walking out the door. He had no idea what changed.

Summer at the lake unfolded in the usual pattern, despite the absence of boats bobbing up and down on the main basin.

31

There was no sand volleyball played at the beach, early sun bathers, or kids making castles with colorful buckets. The championship-level golf course still had a steady stream of golfers cruising around in red carts, knocking balls into and out of the rough and buying drinks from the high school girls who circled the fairways on drink carts; all the same as it was year in and out, except for the noticeable halo the community kept around the water's edge.

The wildlife didn't mind. Sans anxiety, whitetail deer, beaver, and woodchuck descended from the trees to drink. Geese, ducks, coots, cormorant, and seagulls circled and lighted on the traffic-free water. The honks, quacks, and chirps that sounded back and forth between the coves and corridors could only be described as pleased.

* * *

Another quiet week and people began to think Big Todd was a misunderstanding. An embodiment of folklore taken too seriously by unserious people. That thing that happened to the friend of the cousin that everybody swore was true. And then, one day in mid-June, in the middle of Boulder Cove, the crocodile surfaced, in plain sight, and gobbled three mallards who were swimming in a straight line next to Herman Gallaher's floating dock. Pandemonium. A shockwave of froth and blood. The surviving ducks, completely beside themselves, burst into the air, wings buzzing and bills pointing like arrowheads toward the horizon. One duck, under intense stress from the attack, flew directly into the heart of a weeping willow, killing itself. Waves from the assault rippled to shore.

Several witnesses corroborated: Crocodile. Not bullshit. Real. Big. Grayish-green. Massively mouthed. Teeth on top of teeth. The atmosphere full of feathers and noise. But the lake, once settled, dreadfully still. Like a crime scene, cleared and taped off.

Most who lived there knew the water had enough vegetation and mud to grant a creature like Big Todd an opaque unpredictability. In a matter of seconds, a crocodile could be literally out of the water and then back in.

"I'm not sensationalizing. All I'm saying is this god-damned animal can strike wherever and whenever it wants," one of the witnesses said at the emergency townhall forum. Another said, "I read these things can develop a taste for human blood."

Carol, who worked at animal control, sat near the front of the conference room next to the city manager and two members of the city council. She had called the emergency townhall forum. Or, at least, it had been mostly her idea. One of the city council members used the phrase "damage control" while the other said something about "letting the people feel their fears are being heard." The mayor was vacationing in Florida and could not be present. At least forty people attended.

The majority of the townhall was spent by Carol explaining what an animal does and what an animal doesn't do. She never liked how people expected things from animals that were outside of their nature. Why shouldn't a crocodile have a taste for blood? That's how it survived millions of years. And animals don't single out families, or children, or hold grudges, or have feelings, or sense anxieties or weaknesses. They can't smell babies. Or, maybe they can, but they don't think of babies as dessert. Every creature is protein. It's a food source, a way to keep going. That's all an animal lives for. The next day. The next meal. The chance to prolong its life.

After forty-five minutes of testimony, it became clear that the town (at least those in attendance) were split into three factions. About half the attendees wanted Big Todd to be hunted and euthanized in a humane fashion. Another contingency (much smaller) wanted the crocodile to be captured and sent to a regional zoo. The third group, and by far the most enthusiastic, had done research online, and had determined the only way to bring down a saltwater crocodile of significant size was to use dynamite, as fishermen did sometimes in the Philippines when a croc terrorized a coastal village.

* * *

Reynolds, who worked with Carol, was nothing if not true to form. He loved the idea of blowing up Big Todd with dynamite. He blew up things all the time in his backyard. "Artifacts," he called them. Mostly dolls and figurines he bought at garage sales and swap meets. Old televisions and stereo equipment. One time a four-tier wedding cake he paid the town baker five dollars for, even though it was about to be thrown in the dumpster. When the cake exploded it was like magnificent snowballs in a thousand directions. It was a privilege, he thought, to detonate and unravel a thing back to the building blocks of its matter. A definitive blaze of glory. The proper-ist of proper funerals.

He explained this to Carol, but all she did was look at him and say, "Jesus Christ" like she always did.

Reynolds' mom, who housed and cooked for Reynolds, and bought him most of his fireworks, blamed herself for her son's shortcomings. The fact that he didn't seem interested in bettering himself, or seeking an education or career, or even searching for emotional or physical love. Since childhood, he was always off in his own world, ever fascinated by garages and storage rooms and barns full of junk. She never taught him what was safe and what was dangerous. She thought, maybe, he intrinsically knew, how sometimes boys know, intuitively, what makes machines go or how puzzles fit together. But one day, seven-year-old Reynolds walked up to her lawn chair and mentioned, in an offhand way, that he had taken a drink of paint thinner. He enjoyed how paint thinner smelled—like fruit picked from tall treetops—so he had drunk a mouthful. His mom called Poison Control, and then an ambulance, and then, unable to wait another moment, she sped down the highway with her child in lap, praying to a god that had never before helped her.

The shaggy-haired boy insisted he was fine. His stomach didn't even hurt. At Guthrie County, the attending physician ran every bloodwork test under the sun but found no toxicity. It was a minor miracle, or, at least, a close call.

One of the night nurses mentioned, in passing, that she heard ingesting a caustic substance could cause long-term brain or personality disorders. Reynold's mom, drowning in guilt, would forever take the word "could" to mean "would."

* * *

At night, high schoolers from the region cruised the lake's perimeter searching for glowing eyes. Because crocodiles saw in the dark, their eyes became two large reflectors. After sunset, crocs rested in the shadowy water, arms and legs limp, mouths slack, heartrates like drips. "Pretty much fatties floating there," one particularly brave high school boy named Brad said.

He and a large gathering of his classmates had decided, despite the perceived danger, to throw a beach party at Boulder Cove, complete with bonfire and cases of beer. The brave kid was standing, ankle deep, in the water, shining his iPhone flashlight across the cove. The rest of his classmates remained on shore. Most of them wondered what it would be like if Brad got mauled at the edge of the swimming area, right there in front of them. Not that they were worried, but they didn't want to miss it if it happened.

Nobody was interested in going into the lake except Brad, who ventured out to the depth of his thighs. Always ready to fight something that wasn't there, he yelled, "I'll turn you into boots, ya fuckin' lizard."

Brad liked being the only one in the water. The rest of his classmates—total chickenshits. They should remember him this way, in the forefront, tall and unafraid. The moon glowing down on him.

Snorting, Brad slapped the water, egging on whatever lay beneath. He had drunk enough Bud Light Limes that his head felt full of steam. Behind, high school students chattered. Telling him he was a moron, that he was going out too far. Laughter. Jeers. That he was about to get his ass chomped.

"Everybody shut up," someone said. "I see eyes."

* * *

So what happened, then, when Brad saw a crocodile in the water with him, was he started to cry. Big Todd, floating in the night about fifteen feet from where the high schooler waded, wasn't there to devour him, but the high schooler didn't know this. The high schooler hadn't cried in a long time. Not since his dad had taken him for a drive into the country gravel by the Audubon fairgrounds, and told him that he had fallen in love with an old girlfriend from high school, and that he would be leaving Brad and his mom to start a new life. It wasn't a planned thing. But as time marched on, Brad's mother became more and more worn out. The love between Brad's mom and dad frayed. At first on the edges. Then in the middle. Like carpet continually stretched over floorboards that are a step too wide. And this new woman—who really was from the past—was a better future for Brad's father. She wasn't worn. She was bright and surprising in many ways, and she made Brad's father feel alive again when so many other days he felt anything but. Brad, fourteen years old and thinly muscled from playing JV football, struck his father with an open hand, above the ear. "You coward," he said. He had meant for it to be a punch, but, at the last moment the absurdity of what he was doing (trying to knock the lights out of his own father who was twice his size) overwhelmed him, and he unclenched his fist to soften the blow. His dad didn't retaliate to the stinging slap, only turned toward the window. "It will happen to you, too, some day," his father said. "My brother. My dad. Your cousins. All of us Roth boys, unable to stay. It's in our bloodstream. We can't help ourselves." Fourteen-year-old Brad had cried then, inhaling through his nostrils with an angry determination not to sob—to never be anything like his father. Two Roths, staring at the glass across from each other because they couldn't look anywhere else. Frozen in time.

Back at the lake, Brad was also frozen. This time from bone-chilling fear. The closest he had been in his life to danger. His father gone. His mother elsewhere. A man-eating animal three strides away. He had heard of this happening. Mountain climbers frozen on a rock face. A child paralyzed at the sight of a snapping dog. He imagined himself tougher than this, more resilient. But that wasn't him. The real him was frozen knee-deep in the water, crying softly. Waiting to die.

He felt arms pulling him from behind. His elbows. His torso. Dragging him to shore. My boys, he thought. My beautiful boys saving my life.

* * *

Carol was flummoxed. She had Googled and called a person at random—a professor—from some Mickey Mouse college in Florida, during online office hours, and the professor had gone on and on about how Big Todd couldn't be a "saltie." This professor kept using the word "saltie." A Nile crocodile was possible, not even unheard of, but "God damn it, you wouldn't get a saltie all the way up there." Carol didn't know how to respond to the professor other than to say, over and over, that a kid "literally got ate" and she didn't care so much what species the crocodile was, or how many teeth it had. She needed to know how she and Reynolds were going to get the beast out of the water. Alive or dead didn't matter.

"Well, you'll never take it alive," the professor said.

Carol had been dreaming about Big Todd lately. Strange, confusing dreams. Like she was standing outside her parents' house, wearing a little girl's yellow dress. Pigtails again, ribbons in her hair. Big Todd was in the front yard, hunched beneath the American sycamore. He had a red balloon tied around his massive neck. Her hands felt for the rough wood of the picket fence next to her dad's old Impala. She pulled open slowly the gate allowing a pathway for the crocodile to come strolling through, which he did, tongue lolling, the balloon hovering above his head.

There were other dreams, too. A bonfire on Boulder Beach. The townspeople, stripped down to their underwear, roasting an enormous crocodile on a spit. Tearing pieces off and feeding each other. Gorging on reptile meat. In another: Big Todd loped like a bloodhound through the halls of Westside Elementary. Teachers and students screamed and fell all over themselves to get out of his way. The crocodile sniffed discarded backpacks and reams of lined paper. Clawed and shouldered desks and chairs. He swallowed a peanut butter and jelly sandwich that fell from someone's lunch pail. The bell rang, causing the croc to perk his head in attention. He opened his mouth. Magnificent waves of ivory teeth. And then he exploded. Like a bomb. One instant, crocodile. The next, pink and green mist.

Carol closed her eyes and said into the phone. "I mean, can I shoot it? If I shoot it in the head will it die?"

The professor went silent for a long time, and then said, "You don't think it will move on."

"I'm not sure," Carol said. "I don't think so."

The professor said, "They have a small brain. No bigger than a ping pong ball. You'd need a scope. Aim for the spine, immediately behind its head. If you sever the cord, it won't suffer. Make no mistake, though. If you miss, it'll be coming for you directly."

Throughout the phone conversation, Reynolds stood next to Carol's desk with his arms folded, doing his best to eavesdrop. When she hung up, he uncrossed his arms and pushed his hands deeply into jean pockets. She sighed in a long and exasperated way.

"I don't know," she said.

"You know," he said. "You hem and haw about it, but you know."

"Alright," she said. "We can try the dynamite."

"Are you sure?"

"No, I'm not sure at all. And that makes me feel sick."

Reynolds rapped the desk with his knuckles. He smiled and said in a soft voice, "Boss, this is the right thing."

* * *

The Nest (simply called "the bar" by everyone in town) had one topic of conversation. Patrons who ordered a pitcher or played darts or ate jalapeno poppers weighed in on what it would take to eliminate a saltwater crocodile, and, furthermore, who in the room was ruthless enough to do so.

38

On the wall, there was a map of the lake with green push-pins inserted into each spot where Big Todd had been sighted. All residents had received a flier in their mailbox forbidding the hunting of all species of crocodile. Poachers would be prosecuted. Highly illegal, said the flier. But, more importantly, extremely dangerous. The words "extremely" and "dangerous" were double-underlined.

Most evenings in the bar, despite the flier, would consist of someone getting a rabble going. They would move face-to-face, trying to gather a posse of brave souls.

"Tonight's the night."

"I'm in if John goes."

"Let's stop talking about it and do it already."

"My car needs gas, though."

By 9 or 10, the clientele was usually whipped into a frenzy. But as each night waned, so did confidence and enthusiasm. By 11:30, thirty minutes till close, everybody was content to sit in front of the oversized windows, sipping beer and staring out. Re-evaluating, they said.

Across the town square and through six hundred feet of trees was the water's edge. None of them could see it, but they knew it was there. Closer than they wanted it to be.

* * *

Mary Jo Ford wasn't ridiculous, even though people called her that behind her back. Sometimes to her face when they wanted to hurt her. She acted ridiculously sometimes. Behaved ridiculously. Said ridiculous things. Let ridiculous ideas fall from her mouth and onto the carpet with all the ridiculous people she hung out with. Her friends still liked to get drunk, most nights. Ridiculously drunk. And play ridiculous games like Spin the Bottle and Truth or Dare, and, if they got wound up enough, see each other without their shirts on, or their pants, or whatever amount of nakedness they were ridiculous enough to endure on that particular weekend. It was always the same show. Adam Snow would be there with his dark hair and even darker eye-

39

brows. Tina, Brett, Danie with her absurd, fake boobs, Peyton and her weepiness. All of Mary Jo Ford's people in one room. Individually they weren't much, but together they could laugh and pretend.

After work, Mary Joe Ford went to the grocery store to buy a bottle of margarita mix and a six pack of hard cider. Always, she would small-talk the cashiers. They knew her name and routine, that she would show up here on Friday nights, and that she would inevitably return for more next week. The younger ones thought it fun to party. The older ones didn't judge. A train of customers stretched ahead and behind her. Most were buying in bulk.

Long lines at the checkout counter are a reason to behave, she thought. She had read that somewhere, years ago in a book she couldn't remember.

The man in front of her had the look and size of a trucker, his face a maze of creases and acne scars. He had a cart with a single item—a case of Busch Light. The menthol scent coming from his skin and clothing overwhelmed the air between them.

After a while, he said, "Doesn't it feel like a night when things happen?"

He wasn't talking to her. Not really. More like he was thinking aloud, or muttering to himself.

"Things happen every night," said Mary Jo Ford.

The man turned and stared. Then he spun back around, as if embarrassed to have had his voice heard.

After paying for the booze, Mary Jo Ford pushed her cart outside toward her Civic. The man followed, ten steps behind, his menthol smell present even outdoors. She could tell he wasn't parked by her. It wasn't the first time in her life a man had followed her.

The parking lot was filled with cars, and even though the sun was setting, there was plenty of daylight, which gave her courage.

Halfway through the first aisle, she turned on the sole of

her tennis shoe and got right in the man's face. She said, "Dude, you are about two seconds away from being pepper sprayed."

"Take it easy," said the man.

"What the fuck do you want?" She was good at making her voice sound like a ticking time bomb.

"I need to show you something."

Mary Jo Ford nearly laughed. She said, "I don't want to see your dick, mister."

"I get it," the big man said. "You've sized me up, and I don't look right. I drive truck. I tower over people, but I'm telling you right now that what I have to show you is worth seeing."

"I don't recognize you. I don't know you."

The man placed his palms upward, as if in surrender.

"I don't know you either, lady. But I'm not dangerous.

The last punch I threw was in third grade. I've gone to church. I've found God at times. Other times, I have not found God. But I remain hopeful. I have a wife, and three sisters in law. I have nephews and nieces. I don't have business with you or your town. I am passing through this place and nothing more."

"What if I don't want to see what you have to show me."

"Somebody must."

"But why is that somebody me?"

"Because," the man said. "It's necessary that somebody knows what I've done. And you're standing right here."

Mary Jo Ford bit her lip. She wasn't afraid. The man couldn't follow her if she continued to her Civic. Donny was outside, the dumpy manager of the grocery, chatting near the entryway with one of his buddies. All she had to do was scream, and whatever was happening would be over. But she wanted to know what the man intended to show her. She had no clue why it was important. If she drove off and found her friends, and they did the same thing they always did, the man's secret would eat at her for the rest of the night. She might go years, wondering. Her entire life.

"Alright," she said. "Show me."

At the edge of the lot, the man's unmarked 18-wheeler was parked. He undid the latches and spread the double doors on

41

the back of the load. Sunlight flooded into the trailer, which was stacked with blue pallets of regular and Diet Pepsi two-liters. In front of the soda, curled in on itself, was a dead crocodile.

Mary Jo Ford couldn't stop herself. She stepped back, her breath catching in her throat. But then she looked closer and was able to step forward.

A puddle of dark blood pooled in front of the crocodile's mouth. Its neck twisted in an impossible angle. A winch chain wrapped around an armpit and a shoulder. She couldn't differentiate its eyes from the scales on its head, or if the lids were simply closed. The creature was still, too still to be alive, or faking, or whatever crocodiles did when they were playing dead. Its thick arms, legs, and tail. All limp.

"I hit him on 44," the man said. "He was just sitting there, in the highway. A lost king on the road. Isn't he magnificent?"

She didn't respond for a while. Emotion welled inside of her. Relief, maybe. Unwinding fear? Disbelief? More than anything it felt like cold anger, spreading from the center of her into her extremities.

When she finally felt like talking, the first thing she thought to say was, "Dead."

"I killed him."

"You didn't kill him," she said. "You had an accident."

* * *

At 9AM the next day, Reynolds drove Carol to the west side of the lake, past the par 3 golf course that only kids and seniors played—the grounds poorly maintained and ratty in comparison to the championship-level holes on the richer, east side. A steel box in the truck bed held seven sticks of dynamite. He and Carol were on their way to locate Big Todd, and if they tracked him to a particular section of water, they were going to detonate sticks of dynamite under the surface of the lake. Big Todd was already dead, of course, run over by a semi-truck. But they didn't know that yet. Instead, Reynolds felt an immense buoyancy. Like he was floating away into the stratosphere and looking

42

down at himself through the windshield. A euphoria. The pride of knowing one was undertaking an important action. A duty of self-actualization. Something bigger than the self. Stronger than anything he could think of, even his mom's love. His moment was arriving. His eyes were open. Without realizing, he grasped Carol's left hand with his right.

She stared at their intertwined fingers. "I'm sorry," he said, releasing her hand. "I don't know what is happening."

"I don't know what is happening either."

He turned back to the road, steering around the bend.

"That didn't mean anything," he said. "I like you. I have always liked you. I'm not escalating, though. I don't know what to say. This is an important day. And here you are with me. Together we're driving."

"It's okay, Reynolds."

"Man," he said. "I'm not making sense. Man. I do like you, Boss. I don't like a lot of people. I know how I am. But it's such an important day. And I don't feel like I am in control."

"Do you want me to drive?"

"That's not it," he said. "I know what to do. I know exactly what I have to do. I can do this."

"Reynolds, it's okay," she said again.

He looked over to see her outstretched hand. It took him a second to realize she was reaching for his.

2.

Palestine Boy

HE IS RUNNING AROUND the high school track. He is wearing sweatpants and a hood, breathing air wet with September drizzle, legs in steady motion, shoulders relaxed. Cross-country practice has been over for an hour, but still he runs, another ten miles---another forty laps, until the sun sets. His face tells a story. The stitch of his eyebrows, eyes the color of sandalwood, olive skin, cheekbones that curve softly toward a square jaw, puffed nose, his mother's sense of pride, black hair that hangs in tendrils, a peach fuzz beard by the end of the day though he's only seventeen, the way he doesn't flinch when people call him names like "Palestine Boy," "Sandbox," and "Camel."

In Ramallah, where his cousins live, the air isn't wet like this. Nights in the West Bank do not grow quiet, unwind, and fall still. His cousins can outrun him; they are light-boned like gazelles, but he can go farther. In Iowa, he keeps running. They duck into West Bank alleyways or crawl under parked cars. He doesn't break step; they stop and hide. Another lap. Another mile. On the track, a new leg begins where the other ends. The lanes are poorly maintained, bits of black gravel and tire shavings. His shoes are worn. His feet are numb. On the other side of the fence, empty bleachers line the west side of the track. On the other side of the wall, red-tiled roofs.

Later that night, his parents say, go outside, feed the

lambs then make sure to eat, eat until you are full. Eat so your muscles don't waste away like grain piles in the wind. Eat, boy, eat. Fresh greens, rice, vinaigrette salad with almonds and olives, cucumbers, tomatoes, chicken with yogurt---food that makes you strong and fast. Food that keeps you healthy, lean, and proud in your skin.

Silas Jones says that Palestine Boy will put explosives in the school's basement. He will stand on the orange floor of the gymnasium with his arms raised while smoke and fire flow through the hallways and the light fixtures and ceilings fall like big drops of rain. All the students will die when the bomb goes off, he says, and their killer will bury himself in their grave. Silas listens closely when people talk. He waits for them to say something wrong, something that allows him to hit their face. You and homework, Silas, that's a laugh. Isn't your father in jail, Silas, Daddy in the state pen? Doesn't your mom work the streets at night? Doesn't she charge an hourly rate? Doesn't she, Silas? He reaches back, not so much to strike the face but more to strike the voice inside, the mouth, the shaping tongue and lips, the lungs that move air, the mind that constructs sentences. He hits and they reel. When they snap back, come forward with fisticuffs, Silas hits them again---hits them until they are quiet and down for good.

Palestine Boy's cousins throw rocks at the Israeli Army after a Special Forces strike. It's a game, they write to him in their letters, a game the army plays after taking one of our uncles. They don't want us to notice he's gone, so they pick a fight. We throw our rocks, and they shoot their rubber bullets, their canisters that make people cry. Then we run. We run until they catch us, until we are quiet and down for good, or until we get away long enough to play again.

Silas Jones starts for the varsity football team at left guard. In the weight room, he smells the sweat of his teammates, hears the clink of metal against metal, the breathing of the cross-country team doing wall sits on the far side. Palestine Boy is there, Sandbox, Camel, his thin legs bent in ninety-degree angles like

46

3:30 on a clock. The cross-country team shakes in the knees and thighs, all except him. He is steady, like the support spike of a fence driven deep into dirt. He is the lead runner but not the captain, the first one across the finish line but not the first congratulated. Did he run fast enough to make us win? the team wants to know. Did we have the best cumulative time? Silas bench presses 275 pounds four reps before he is winded. The center spots him, and Silas muscles out the fifth, groans loud enough for the room to hear. He locks eyes with Palestine Boy when he sits up, lets him know that he is stronger, that he is muscle and power and authority---he is the ability to push someone into spaces they don't want to go, the ability to block defensive linemen and linebackers, blitzing cornerbacks, anything that tries to get past him.

He is always facing a wall, Palestine Boy. The fence behind his house. The walls of the bus that takes him to high school. The space between him and the other faces at the lunch table, the hallways, the locker rooms, the drop-ceiling above, the tile below, the stones that circle school grounds, the letters his cousins send him from overseas. Always a wall.

The wall in his cousin's letters stands twenty-five feet high---twenty-five steps between the face of the wall and their back door. Palestine Boy's youngest cousin wants to see the Mediterranean before she turns thirteen; she wants to travel east on a bus like they used to, and float in the Dead Sea where the air smells like salt and the water is so dense she can't go under. She wants to visit her friends in Amman, where there are no walls and checkpoints and machinery that yells in the night when she should be asleep.

After he graduates, Silas Jones plans to drive his Chevy S10 up to Anchorage, Alaska, where it is cold nine months of the year, and a man of considerable size and strength is not an anomaly. When he closes his eyes, he imagines a place that smells of fish, cold sweat, and decades of snow; a place that sounds like locomotives winding through mountainsides and pitchforks ringing off gold bullion; a place that is home to timber wolves, grizzly bears, and men that live like flashes of lightning.

47

Silas' mom tells him he is eating too much. "You need to slow down," she says. "I can't be running to the grocery store every day just to keep you fed." Silas grows angry when he hears this. She doesn't understand how the extra weight helps, how it makes him harder to penetrate, gives him the extra push he needs to keep the defense on their side of the line. How it allows him to enforce order. She doesn't understand that size defines him.

Palestine Boy wants, more than anything, to be disconnected from his people's problems. He wants his mother to smile when she hangs up the telephone. He wants his father not to smoke a pack of Lucky Strikes during the national news. He wants to make love to a pretty girl underneath a blanket, win the state cross-country meet, and be scouted by east-coast schools. If he could lie in an empty field, arms and legs spread like making a snow angel---nothing around for miles except grass and wind and cirrus clouds---that would be enough. For now, though, he settles on a warm shower after an evening run. He rests his face in the crook of his arm, leans against the wall, the stream of water down his shoulders and back. He twists the dial left and right, slowly---cold to hot, hot to cold. The frigid water chills his skin, so cold it hurts, but the relief of warm water makes the pain worthwhile. It makes everything better. It becomes his concentration, his meditation, cold to warm, hot to cool, a reason to keep going, keep breathing, keep running toward the next mile's end.

In the locker room, Silas Jones steps on the doctor's scale. The balance beam clinks, flush against the bottom. He pushes the toggle all the way to the right, 350 pounds. The beam rises slowly and rests against the top. He adjusts the scale to 335, then 337. The beam wavers and stabilizes.

He stares at the numbers, hopes that football season will be over before he breaks 350. The coaches will have to estimate his heaviness then, or maybe bring in a bigger scale just for him. He turns. Other athletes are lined up behind him. Everyone must weigh in before the weekend. The next in line is Palestine Boy.

He is standing, shirtless. Long, smooth muscles fill his legs, but his chest is flat. Stripes of ribs push out his sides, between his nipples.

Silas understands that Palestine Boy will never deal with the problems that he will likely suffer. Silas is mostly muscle, but after college he will face obesity, heart disease, arthritis. For now, football keeps him healthy, but he knows that muscle turns to fat when given too much rest. He runs a hand over his own chest, dense flesh and hair. He wishes he could control his eating, wishes he could stay fit for the rest of his life.

"Let me put this on pussy weight," he says. He adjusts the scale to 50 pounds and steps off.

On hot September afternoons, Palestine Boy trains at pace speed on gravel roads. It is too humid for a shirt, but he wears one anyway. Fabric, salt water, and dust cling to his skin. If he follows the gravel, he can continue to the next town, Low Moor, and then maybe Cambridge. Keeping off the main highways, he runs past yapping farm dogs, peeling barns, and goldening fields. Men in bandanas and blue jeans ride monstrous combines and tractors through soybeans. They raise a hand in greeting as he passes. That boy runs like crazy, the farmers say. Saw him the other day down near Whitehorse. That's twelve miles from school. Twenty-four round trip. Got a real chance to get his college paid for, maybe even win state is what I hear.

In their letters, his cousins say, The soldiers are not all bad people. We play football in the dirt field next to the guard towers. Sometimes they clap when we score goals, throw a Hershey bar to the MVP. If you ask them a question in English, they usually talk. They like Italian football. They follow it close, tell us who is hot and who is cold. There's one soldier, a light-haired guy about your age, who says he was born in Kansas, America. He might even be our friend. He doesn't agree with the things the army does, but he has no choice. "Orders are orders," he tells us. "Why can't people our age make up our own minds? Why are we made to fight a war our grandparents started?" We don't know what to say to him when he talks like this, but we listen.

Grandmother says our old life ended with the wall. She won't look at it anymore. When she walks down the street to market, she holds a hand beside her face to block the sight. She comes home through narrow stone streets, where the path is slick with oil and puddles, and the buildings are too tall to see above. If she talks about it, she won't say "the wall" or "the fence." She says "the end of the world." We painted the section outside our house, Grandmother's words in big block letters. That is the first thing you see out the back door. "The end of the world." Did we mention the wall is snake-like? That's the shape it makes, a big curving S like a mouse-hunting viper, winding its way through Ramallah. Your youngest cousin wants to know: Can you really run from town to town in America? You don't have to get a pass? You don't have to stand in line and wait for months? And what is it like to live in a wood house? Are there rats? Will your house blow away in strong wind or rot in a rainstorm? Why do Americans build with sticks and branches what we have built for thousands of years with stone?

Nighttime at the farm. Palestine Boy wets his finger. Inside the perimeter of the electric fence, the lambs run in and out of the barn like children playing tag in the floodlights. One second, they are out in the yard staring intently, the next they are sprinting toward the safety of their pens. Palestine Boy touches his spit to the wire. The current runs through and he pulls back, wringing out his hand. From over by the power source, his father says in English, "That's the low setting. Just a whisper that means stay away."

"It's on. I felt it."

"Good, it still works," his father says. He almost never speaks Arabic anymore. "The lambs were scratching their haunches against it the other day. I thought it had shorted out in last week's frost. I'll turn the volts up, maybe."

Palestine Boy scoops handfuls of oats from the trough. He holds them over the fence. The lambs trot over excitedly. They lap the oats from his palms with thick, dry tongues. When his hands are empty, they bleat for more. He raises his arms in apology, but the night is hot and they are irritable. They continue to whine, continue to beg for more handfuls. Their eyes are dark and wet, their tone insistent. When he pockets his hands, the lambs snort and race back to the barn. In the floodlights, they are flashes of white on top of shadows.

After cross-country practice, Palestine Boy stretches his legs in preparation for his track workout. Silas Jones walks up to the chain-link fence. He hangs his shoulder pads and football helmet on the post. "Coach decided you need to teach me to run," he says. "I need to be fast like you are. I can't be like my brothers."

Palestine Boy stretches his hamstring. He touches his toes, then bends farther until his knuckles are flat on the ground. Silas says, "You probably don't know. One of my brothers played guard at USC and the other went to Michigan, but they're fat now that football's over. Fat in the heart. Morbidly obese. Coach says they're going to have heart attacks like my gramps did, and my gramps' brothers. They're going to die before 55. Coach doesn't want that to happen to me, so he sent me over here to train with you."

Palestine Boy stands up. He meets Silas' green eyes, doesn't know if he should trust him. "You can run with me," he says, "but those cleats will hurt your feet."

Silas removes his shoes and socks. He sets the shoes next to the post and drapes his socks over the fence. "I'll just run on the grass, then, right along the track. I can't get too skinny. Got me a football scholarship to Kansas State. I just need to be a little faster, a little leaner. That's all I'm after."

They jog several laps around the track. Silas struggles. He runs with tight shoulders, toes, and fists. His breath comes heavy like a big farm dog's. Every time he catches up, Palestine Boy increases speed. Silas tries to keep pace, but slows at the end of lap three. "Hold on," he says. "I got a side stitch. Let's walk a lap."

He puts his hands behind the back of his head, coughs, and sucks air. His face is red and the top of his t-shirt is wet. He says, "You get a running scholarship anywhere?"

51

"I haven't heard anything, yet."

"Probably will, though, right?"

"I don't know."

"Can I ask something?" Silas says. "I mean, something that might offend you---but it shouldn't, because I don't mean nothing by it. I just want to know. Mind if I ask something like that?"

"Okay."

"Think you would've got a scholarship by now if you were a white?"

Palestine Boy rolls his head back, touches each shoulder with an ear. He looks off into the distance, toward the cornfields. He doesn't feel like giving an answer. "Maybe. I try not to think about that."

"Look," says Silas. "I didn't mean nothing by it. I was just curious. You think I hate Middle Easts and Blacks and Hispanics, but that's not really true. I just wish that people would leave each other alone, you know. I wish people over there wouldn't kill each other all the time, stop setting off bombs and burning oil fields, stuff like that."

Silas stops walking. He bends over, hands on his knees. Palestine Boy waits, stepping from foot to foot, as Silas breathes and spits in the grass. He wipes his mouth and straightens up.

"This isn't coming out right," he says. "All I'm saying is that it's shitty when people associated with you mess things up. It's shitty that my brothers are so fat, and Coach automatically thinks I'm going to be the same way. It's shitty that I'm out here, with you, running laps after practice because of them. That's what I'm saying. It's shitty."

Palestine Boy looks away. He says, "Are you ready to start again?"

"Give me a minute. How many miles you run, anyway?"

"I go until I get tired."

Silas shakes his head. He spits. "Must be a long way."

We miss you when you aren't here, the cousins say in their most recent letter. We miss you and Aunt and Uncle.

Grandmother says don't worry about us. Palestine won't fall down. When we talk about the bad times, it only lasts a moment. It's like a passing breeze, touches us just for a second, and then it's flying again, off to the Mediterranean. If you look one way, you see the wall, Grandmother says, but the other way is the streets of Palestine, friends, and the morning sun coming to warm you.

When he and Silas begin to jog again, Palestine Boy sees, above the fence, the bricks of the school rise over the red-seated bleachers. The flat, gravel roof. Above that, a church's slender steeple. High-rise grain elevators with blue catwalks in-between. The spikes of two radio towers. To the left of the parking lot, past the flagpole, he sees a harvested field, stripped bare of spring wheat and corn. On both sides of the field, unpicked crops frame its emptiness, its flatness. The open, harvested stretch continues into the distance, beyond the walls of yellow corn and wheat stalks, to a place where he cannot tell a difference between the clouds and the horizon.

As they round the corner, he realizes he is looking east.

Bubbleheads

JENNY AND SUNNY DECIDED to drive down Carrico Road because why not.

Somewhere lost in the woods between Saint Louis and the Missouri River lived the Bubbleheads. Everybody knew the stories—a disfigured family with jack-o-lantern-wide skulls. Warts and lumps and tumors and hair follicles. Puss and dandruff and God-knows-what-else. Maybe the mouth isn't where it's supposed to be. Maybe there's a third nostril over by the ear. Extra skin surrounding an eye swollen to the size of a chicken's egg. What would these Bubbleheads do if they fell upon two young girls who had just received their driver's licenses? What if the car broke down at the end of the gravel road? Jenny didn't know the answers to these questions, but her skin prickled at the thought of terrible, wide faces flying by the window glass.

Sunny said, "I'm going to hold your hand. And I want you to turn off the headlights."

Jenny (who was in love with Sunny though she could never say the words aloud) did as she was told, pressing the brake and pulling to the edge of the gravel road.

"No, no," Sunny said, squeezing Jenny's hand. "Not like that. Keep driving."

"But how will I see?"

"Use your instincts. Your eyes will adjust."

"Alright," said Jenny.

With the headlights off, the road ahead became nothing. Blankness framed by the ghosts of tree limbs.

"That's it. Now go faster. Really push yourself."

Jenny did her best to stay in the center of the dark gravel. She could hear the tires churning through rock and dirt. A dim sense of danger simmered in her stomach. She should have been steering with two hands, but Sunny's palm felt nice under hers, and this was as close to intimacy as they'd been. A thought crept through her mind: An important moment between the two of them might be passing.

A loud snap and the car pulled sharply left. Something under the tire. Jenny released Sunny's hand and pushed the brake down as hard as she could. The vehicle fishtailed to a stop, and she flicked on her headlamps. Dust and tree trunks a mere six feet from the bumper.

"You ran over a big stick," said Sunny. "You might have to get out and change a flat tire."

"That's not funny."

"It's kind of funny."

Both girls stopped talking. In the silence, Jenny's breath came in staccato bursts, but she wouldn't let herself cry. Instead, she said, "Everything out of your mouth is a joke. Nothing matters to you. A person can't really know you because you never say what you actually think about anything."

Sunny looked out the window into the night and said, "I'm thinking about the Bubbleheads living in this woods. I'm thinking about how they want to eat us alive."

Spectacular Regular

THE DISTURBED MAN CRESTS on the blue, iron bridge. He's unloading rounds at passing cars. Active, they call him, though he is standing still, not aiming. He squeezes the trigger, shakes his head, and then squeezes. Again and again. Leavenworth, Kansas on the near bank. A military base facing a prison described as The Hot House. On the far side, sloped Loess Hills. The broadleaved outskirts of Weston Bend State Park. Clouds fast-moving overhead. Underfoot, the heavy current of the Missouri River. Cobwebs on the bridge. The cars stick in the strands. The cars break free. The spiders are everywhere. An infestation, milling. Dangling from the truss. And then a vehicle. Too close to be real. Too close to be. For a moment, man and vehicle become one object. And then: Spinning tops. A dreidel on an oak table. Silver tornadoes. A maelstrom catching ships with giant sails. Quicksand hardening in the sun. A face on the bridge. Blinking up.

There are cities that never burn, and leaves that bob slowly on the ocean surf. There is blond sand that one can sink their feet into, ankle deep, and purple mountains in the backdrop. Ski towns and log cabins. Curfews nonexistent. Simmering in the hot tub—witnessed by a million stars—a hand reaches into the snow. Underneath the cold, a neck of sparkling wine. In this place, every time someone falls in love is the first and last time. Ears ring. Strangers burst firecrackers. As night falls, the pavement grows cold. But it's never cold here. And it's never night. And the spiders—always the perfect soldiers—march in single file. They are huge and unimaginable.

Viper

SNAKES OCCASIONALLY SUN THEMSELVES on the bike trail. Garters and ribbons, mostly. Long and fat black snakes. Gray racers. Northern water snakes. Beautiful, striped milk snakes.

The single mother down the hill from me swears there is a cottonmouth living in a cement hole next to the Brookfield trail entrance. "A water moccasin," she calls the snake the second time she brings it up. She and her daughter used to love to go for walks on the bike trail, but you-know-what is standing in the way of her joy. She's asking me to kill the snake, I realize, but also never to tell her about what I've done.

In my running shoes and shorts, I walk to the trailhead that merges with our neighborhood, an old, dusty spade in my left hand. The May weather is just starting to warm—upper seventies today. A chance of eighties tomorrow, and then another storm.

There is no snake. I shine my cellphone light down the hole in the cement. I stamp my feet all around and part the locks of tall grass with the spade handle. Nothing.
I walk a hundred yards down the trail, and then a hundred up. It's probably just an everyday water snake the single mother saw. It's easy to confuse the two if you don't know what you are looking at.

A couple months pass before I think of the snake again. The calendar says July and I am running on the trail in 90 plus degree heat. From the bottom of the Prairie Creek Greenway to our housing development is a mile-long rise. It's a killer hill, especially since I always try to push my last mile. I finished second in my age division in the Midnight Madness 10K—thirteen seconds behind the leader— and I don't want to get that close this year and not win.

I had assured the single mother the cottonmouth (if it even existed) was surely dead or moved on. All those walkers, bikers, and runners. An animal would be terrified to live in that hole.

But the snake is there when I reach the top of the hill. Fat and half-coiled before me with brown and charcoal bands. Its face has pits. I don't need to see its open, white-laced mouth. I can tell by the elliptical pupils—its cat eyes. The single mother is right. This snake is a viper.

I don't know what to do. Here I am, completely spent. No spade in sight. No screaming children running with arms flailing. No victims or witnesses. My hair is wild. Skin bright red. Arms and legs sweat-slick and trembling. The snake and I bake in the sun—in this nearly one hundred degrees of heat pressing down. The two of us are in each other's way, both staring directly into the golden brown eyes of the creature before us.

We can kill each other. Both of us know it. Yet neither one of us can move.

The V Scale

VIOLET HAD NATURALLY STRONG hands. The first time she stepped into a bouldering gym, she gripped her hands around every colorful hold available on the wall. Reaching the top of the twelve-foot plywood was easy, but then she watched the climbers around her and realized that each color represented a route—or "problem." And they weren't just red, yellow, blue, green, and black handles sticking out at strange angles. They were jugs and buckets, and edges, and crimps, and pinches, and slopers, and all kinds of lingo she thought silly on day one but would gradually learn to use over the next nine months.

Most of the problems on the wall were unsolvable. Her grip strength was excellent, and she could do assisted pull-ups at the gym, but her body weight, she figured, was too heavy to excel at this sport. She was drawn to it, though. Not so much the idea of climbing rock faces in daylight, but the trick of solving these indoor, color-coded puzzles of increasing difficulty.

One of the workers at the climbing gym, some college-aged kid, stood under where Violet was working. He clapped softly when she put both hands on a yellow jug with a flag on it—the uppermost hold in the problem.

"A V2 on your first day," he said when she dropped back to the mat. "Do you know how long it took me to climb a V2?"

She smiled and wiped the sweat from her brow with her hand. Her fingers burned. Looking down, she saw that the flesh had been rubbed off on two of her left-hand fingers, and one on her right. She held her palms out for the worker kid to inspect.

"Good," he said. "Everybody needs to leave a little skin on the wall."

"Do I need to stop?"

"Not unless you want to. Your hands will hurt a bit, but you can tape them and keep going. You wiped blood on your forehead, though. You should probably wash that off so you don't look psychotic."

* * *

Violet's first day of bouldering was the day she found out her mother had skin cancer. Two experiences she had trouble separating: Day one of climbing and day one of cancer.

Here's how it happens. Violet was sitting there, ready to chit-chat all evening—chit-chat at Panera like she and her mom always do about people they know who are sleeping around or behaving badly, or her aunt's drinking, or whatever is the drama of the week. But then Violet noticed that her mom was wearing a sizable bandage on her arm, and why would her mother wear such a sizable bandage. Her mom shook her head, as if exasperated by the sight of the dressing, and then she said "It's a melanoma," or maybe she only said "melanoma" without the "it's" or the "a." Violet suddenly couldn't parse words. She said "fuck, shit, Mom" or maybe "shit, Mom, fuck." And then the two women fell into a vicious whispering fight where Violet accused her mother of exaggerating things and not listening to doctors. The dermatologist had probably said it was a carcinoma, or even eczema, but her mother was too flighty or distracted to listen properly to something as serious as a cancer diagnosis. This was normal, dramatic Mom. This was utterly-expected, normal, dramatic Mom bullshit. And Violet couldn't put up with dramatic Mom bullshit. Not tonight.

"Sweetie, calm down," her mom said. "Look at me."

"I don't want to."

"Violet."

"What?"

"They cut it off, V. And they took a big circle around the cancer. The doctor said there's no way it's spread. She's nearly certain. I won't have to do chemo or radiation or anything like that. I just have to go in every three months for a skin check. It's already been solved."

Violet didn't cry at the restaurant because her mother didn't want that. Instead, she bit her lip, and both she and her mom began to eat. Alone after dinner, she drove through the city, listening to the radio and thinking about living the rest of her life without her best friend. And then, when she pulled into the carport of her apartment complex, it started to rain. She thought maybe it was appropriate to sob along with the clouds, but she, for some reason, couldn't. In order to start crying she would have to stop thinking about the spot on her mom's arm, and that seemed impossible.

* * *

At work, when things were slow, Violet would watch Youtube videos of climbers—sometimes in gyms, sometimes on true rock faces. One of her favorites was Adam Ondra's sending of a route he named "Silence" within the mouth of Hanshelleren Cave in Flatanger, Norway. The "Silence" problem—an inverted route to the high point of the cave's ceiling—was rated the first ever 9C in the French grading system, which translated to a maxed-out V17 climb in the V-scale that Violet recognized.

Elite climbing routes were not even attemptable to but a handful of people on the planet. Adam Ondra, Chris Sharma, Lynn Hill, Sasha DiGuilian, Alex Honnold, Catherine Destivelle, and Margo Hayes were names Violet learned through the internet—watching clips and mini-documentaries, reading narratives, looking at images of mountains and routes and climbing competitions set to ridiculous classical music or techno-pop backgrounds.

Who were these people? she wondered as she clicked on video after video. How did they stick to walls so effortlessly? Was there any skin left on their fingers, or was it just calluses on top of bone? Were these climbers anything like her, having had strong hands all their lives but no idea what to use them for?

Six nights a week, a semi-famous boulderer named Tina—nationally ranked by USA Climbing—worked out at Violet's gym. Sometimes two camera operators would film Tina flashing some of the harder problems on the wall put up specifically for her. She was good enough at climbing that people actually paid her to do it. Her gear (and the gear of the camera crew) featured screen-printing and patches from regional sponsors.

Tina was the alpha of the gym. The boss. The undisputed, heavyweight champion. She'd placed in and won climbing competitions in twelve different states. Everybody else in the room was recreational. She was the pro. The other gym-goers would gawk when Tina was around, especially after hearing her scream. Tina didn't scream when she fell, but when she maneuvered between grips, or when she found herself in the pain of an especially small crimp, she would open her mouth and fill the gym with a noise that said stop-what-you-are-doing-and-look-at-me. It wasn't a painful scream as much as a motivational scream. Not anything like those cartoonishly swollen assholes in weight rooms who grunt when they want people to know how much weight they can lift. This was better. More personal. Serious business. She wanted the wall to know she wasn't quitting. She would get back up and complete the problem, no matter how many times she fell. And if she ran out of stamina or strength, she would go home and soak her split fingers in vinegar, and then she would come back the next day and take the problem down. That's what her scream meant. A persistent invincibility. Tina had brown skin and nearly buzzed hair. Violet didn't think the professional boulderer looked all that strong until she caught sight of her clinging to a sloper one evening. Tina's back, while trying not to slip off the hold, flared to almost twice its size. Her build was all shoulders, lats, and trapezius, and she had huge, leathery hands that were covered in chalk. She reached upward and found a better hold, set her feet alongside the sloper, and then hung by her left arm so she could re-chalk her right fingers, and then hung from her other arm to re-chalk the left.

In short: Tina was unrelenting. She was also incredible. And unlike the climbers Violet saw on the internet, Tina was flesh and blood. Violet couldn't believe how enthralled she was. There was such a thing as a climbing crush, and Violet had it bad for Tina. She wished so hard that she could do the things that the stronger woman could do.

One night, the camera crew filmed Tina going after a newly mounted V10 problem. Another climber, Dusty, who had spiked hair and worked in the same building as Violet, stood with her watching.

"Isn't she badass?" Violet said after Tina locked in a difficult knee bar.

"Yes. Totally," said Dusty.

"And beautiful, too. She's strong and beautiful, and she does everything well."

"Jeez. I don't know about that, V."

"Just agree with me, please."

After a while, Dusty said, "Do you really think she's beautiful?"

"Of course. Don't you?"

"I guess so."

"What do you mean you guess so?"

"I just—I have a weird thing. I don't find muscles all that attractive on women."

"You can't be serious."

"Muscles gross me out. I can't explain it."

* * *

Violet feared bouldering outside the confines of the gym. There was a specific sect of climbers, almost entirely male, who were into the thrill of free soloing—essentially climbing to the top of a cliff or mountain without any sort of rope or protection. And it was crazy. And it was stupid. And if these climbers fell then they died—a terribly painful and violent death—which was maybe the most male thing of all time. And Violet didn't want any part of that mindset.

It's okay, she assumed, to climb in the comforts of climate control where the stakes were low. If she fell the wrong way onto the mat she might twist an ankle or sprain a wrist, maybe even break a bone, but her life would continue. She had no interest in dying in the name of a sport, or for passion, or glory, or whatever reason these free-soloing men chose to amuse themselves in death's playground.

Violet had her own brush with mortality when she was seven years old. Bacterial meningitis come close to taking her young life. Kids died of this illness every single year, but she survived.

After soccer practice, she complained of a sore neck. (This was back when kids were still allowed to do headers, and her mom assumed a stiff muscle.) When the young girl awoke in the middle of the night, vomiting, her mom asked again if her neck hurt.

"I can't move my chin at all," said Violet.

Her mom rushed her to the local ER, which sent her by ambulance to the children's hospital downtown for immediate intravenous antibiotics. In route to the hospital, Violet's blood pressure dropped to a dangerously low level, and her body went into shock. There was a ninety minute stretch, her mom told her, where things got especially scary, but even years later, when Violet asked her mom about it, she won't give any more detail.

For two days and two nights, Violet's mom stayed by her daughter's side. She slept in ten to twenty minute stretches, always holding the seven-year-old's hand.
Violet remembered little of the stay in the hospital, but one memory she can recall is opening her eyes to find her mother staring back at her.

* * *

There were young teens at the bouldering gym on Sat-

65

urday—someone's thirteen or fourteenth birthday party. Violet wore a loose-fitting silver tank top and was immediately self-conscious about the amount of skin she might be showing when she clung sideways to the wall, the tank dripping from her shoulders and her teal sports bra in full display. Usually, the gym was populated by legit boulderers—people more interested in the problems on the wall than the bodies climbing them. She didn't trust teenagers, especially boys who hooted each time one of them fell and called each other "pimp" when one successfully scaled the twelve foot plywood. Most of the teens stuck to the VB and V0 problems, though each one attempted, at some point, the impossible V11 in the expert section of the gym that only Tina could climb. Their wiry bodies couldn't even make it off the starting blocks.

She envied the young boys' metabolism, though—their high school skinniness. All her life she had been cognizant of her body. She was, through college and her mid-twenties, a fluctuator. She would move from a healthy weight to twenty pounds over, and then back again. The worst part was her neck. She could always tell her trimness in photographs by looking at her neck fat, even more so than the size of jeans she wore. She hated her neck. It was the ugliest thing about her body.

If she kept a strict diet, and if she exercised, the loose skin would tighten, and her chin would look fine—presentable. If she carried extra weight, though, she was always self-conscious of the puffiness under her throat.

Since becoming serious about climbing, her body had tightened all over. She could see the muscles filling out her frame. She wasn't lifting weights, either, it was entirely the exercise of bouldering. There were people out there who might like the way she looked naked now, who might stare at her without fixating directly on her neck fat.

Violet wondered if Tina noticed her body the way Violet noticed Tina's. She'd been having dreams recently where she and Tina climbed side-by-side on the bouldering wall, the rest of the gym empty. Sometimes in the dreams, Tina would swing on one arm over to Violet's problem. Suddenly, the stronger woman's face was inches from hers. Violet wanted so badly to kiss Tina, but her arms were completely pumped out, and she couldn't pull herself any higher.

When Violet woke from these dreams, she felt frustrated and lonely. She'd slept with men before, several times, but never a woman. She wondered if she'd like it—if she'd rather have a woman's strong hands between her legs than anything a man could offer.

One of the teen boys was trying to flash a V3, and he took a bad angle on a double pinch route high on the wall. She knew what was about to happen. As soon as he shifted the weight off his left foot, he tumbled backwards through the air and crash landed on the mat.

"Charlie, you stupid asshole," one guy yelled from across the room.

Violet released herself from the wall and knelt next to the teen. He was gasping for breath, and there were tears in his eyes. He had landed directly on his back, which meant he probably didn't break anything, but he likely had the wind knocked out of him.

"Can you get up?" she said.

"I don't want to do this anymore," he said.

* * *

Violet's mom seemed to take the cancer diagnosis in stride. Every time her daughter brought it up, she simply blew it off. "It's over and done," she'd say. And then Violet would press about the cancer returning in a different spot, and her mom would tell her that the dermatologists would find the new growth and cut that off too.

Checking her own skin became a daily ritual for Violet, and she went twice in the span of two weeks to the general practitioner to have her moles examined. The most anxious thing about melanoma, she decided, was a person's ability to catch it before it became deadly—as her mother did—and Violet didn't know if she could handle the responsibility of keeping herself alive.

Frustrated at the doctor who assured her the mole on her back was completely benign, Violet stood abruptly from the exam table on her third visit of the month.

"I am not a ridiculous person," she said to the doctor.

"I never said you were," the doctor said back.

"People come in here all the time with this stuff. Like they won't give up until they find something. I'm not like them. I'm just trying to be safe."

The doctor, an older black woman, sat on the office chair by the computer and folded her hands in her lap.

"You know somebody who has got it," she said.

"Got what?"

"Skin cancer. Of course, you do. Otherwise you wouldn't be in here. You'd be out rock climbing and callusing up those pretty hands."

Violet, still standing, stared at the doctor. Then she put her head down and said, "I can't turn it off. Some days it's all I think about."

The doctor patted her hand and said, "Listen. Somebody's got it, but that somebody isn't you. Not right now. You can check yourself. That's good. And if something concerns you, by all means come in and let's take a look. But there are no certainties in life. No amount of doctors can assure a person one hundred percent that they are going to be okay. But you should be okay. You're young and healthy, and that has to be enough for you."

Later, after leaving the clinic, Violet called her mother.

"Hello, there. What is my daughter up to on a Friday night? Heading to the gym?"

"Mom, do you remember when I was little and I got sick in the hospital?"

"Of course."

"I never said thank you."

"For what?"

"For staying with me the whole time. I never said thank you for that."

"That was over twenty years ago. Why are you thinking about that right now?"

"Because I never said it then. And I want to say it before it's too late."

Her mom didn't talk for what seemed two or three minutes. Then she said, "Sweetie, I'm not dying."

Violet tried to say "I never said you were dying," but simply breathed into the phone instead.

* * *

Mountaineering and climbing were intrinsically dangerous, and the sports carried with them grim statistics. Free soloists, in particular, had low life expectancies.

Climbers died regularly on cliffs and mountains. The Annapurna Massif, in the Himalayas, boasted a thirty-three percent kill rate on all people who tried to reach the summit. Kanchenjunga, the third highest mountain in the world behind Everest and K2, buried one in five. La Dura Dura, Mount Fitz Roy, El Capitan, and The Matterhorn have all slaughtered their fair share of men and women who wanted to taste the air on top of the world.

Some climbers reached a summit only to meet their end on the way back down. Some had close calls—surviving by what can only be described as alpine miracles—and then they died the next trip up the mountain, or on some other lonely cliff or snow-worn peak. The majority of climbers lived on, and the survivors threw down the challenge flag for the next person in line.

People, Violet concluded, were stupid. Climbers were some of the most reckless people in the universe. There was something missing inside of them, and this something was replaced by a want to look death straight in the eyes. An unnerving "off-ness" persisted in the faces of free soloists—as if they knew they weren't supposed to live full-length lives. They had spent too much time nearly falling, maybe. One slip of the foot, or one grip going numb, and it was a one-thousand-foot slide down a sheer rock face.

Violet had taken her turns at falling in the climbing gym. The worst time being when she attempted to reach the final hold of a V4 problem and lost her grip on the last move. She burned her legs on the rough wall, and on the way down her arm caught a jug and tore a good chunk of skin off her elbow. Some of the other boulderers surrounded her after the fall, and she lay there gasping and bleeding, just like the teen she stood over who swore off climbing for the rest of his life.

* * *

It was Saturday. The college kids working the front desk at the climbing gym had the hip-hop channel blasting on the stereo. Violet walked past Dusty, the guy with spiked hair who worked in her building and was still plateaued on the V3s, and stood next to the wall that featured V6 and above problems—the place where only experts belonged. Tina was there, dressed in her expensive, sponsored gear, looking beautiful and just kicking everybody else's ass.

Tina, without fanfare, placed both hands on the top of the wall inside the green half-square—the international bouldering competition maneuver that signified a problem's completion—and then dropped the twelve feet back to the mat. She turned and knelt next to her chalk bag.

"You're Tina, right?" said Violet.

The professional climber looked up and said, "Yeah."

"If you don't mind, I'd really like to boulder with you."

Tina rubbed chalk onto her palms and fingers. She said, "What's your name?"

"I usually go by V."

"Alright, V. What level do you climb?"

"I'm trying not to look at the numbers anymore."

Tina smiled and said, "Good girl. Now turn around and let me look at your back."

Violet did as she was told and felt strong fingers touching the muscles alongside her spine. They weren't massaging but searching.

After a few moments she heard Tina say, "There they are."

"What?"

"Your wings. I can feel them."

Liar, Liar

SEVENTEEN-YEAR-OLD BOY on the cross-country team doesn't need as many calories as the overweight fifteen-year-old he was two years ago. On the paved trail, seventeen-year-old boy runs as fast as he can for four miles, with minimal calories consumed, over the six different bridges between Polk City and Madrid, Iowa, and then turns around at the mile marker and runs as fast as he can home. "Stay lean," he repeats to himself. "Stay fast."

Seventeen-year-old boy never wins any sanctioned races, but he letters on the varsity squad and wins a few copper-coated medals. He grows up at some point. He also grows out of whatever phase he was in that made him eat so little and run so much. After earning a degree at the state university, he accepts a position as an underwriter for an insurance agency. He's lucky to land a job right out of school at a stable and recognizable company. The entry-level cohort— Forty strong! The company had such a great year!—participates in get-to-know-you-games on their first day. One game the managers suggest is called "Two truths and a lie." Two women in the cohort claim they survived an eating disorder as one of their "truths," but seventeen-year-old boy is skeptical. Neither was sent, at any point, to the hospital. They never described jumping up and down before throwing up, or the gnawing feeling of starvation, or even the faraway look of their reflection in the mirror. Seventeen-year-old boy finds "Two truths and a lie" to be as fake of a thing as exists in the universe.

When his turn arrives, he says, "I am an only child. My favorite color is black. My favorite color is purple."

* * *

Time passes. Seventeen-year-old boy gets older, gets promoted. Now age 27, he begins to oversee some of the new people at the same stable and recognizable company—Another great year! Not as good as six years ago, but still pretty solid!—and he meets, finally, a girl who hurts herself. Seventeen-year-old boy cannot remember to which team she belongs—Raquel's or Ramona's?—but he sees a girl who hurts herself around the office on Tuesdays and Thursdays during the mid-week huddle. She is younger than him, freckled and pale, and her hair is like a creamsicle waterfall. He doesn't know her secret until the night of the company social, at the British pub downtown. A girl who hurts herself is wearing a purple dress, and he isn't trying to look— Truth: he really is—but when she sits at the high-top, her skirt rides up and he sees the scars. Criss-crosses and lines. Hard, raised skin. All over the front of her thighs. He realizes that she can see him—she can see him seeing her—and she is smoothing the dress back to her knees. She is angry, maybe. Embarrassed, surely. She finishes her drink and stands at the table before swiveling and retreating toward the bar.

Seventeen-year-old boy moves to intercept her. He doesn't mean to be so direct—That's a lie!—but he feels an overwhelming urge to talk to a girl who hurts herself. He extends his hand and says his name and title at the company. Absently squeezing his palm, she leans over the bar and calls her drink order into the chaos before them.

"You're all cut up," seventeen-year-old boy wants to say. He wants to run his fingers along her scars and feel exactly what it is she felt when she hurt herself. He wants to be sad with her, maybe. Save her. Transplant her skin. Hug her. Love her. Cry on her legs. Above all else, he wants to look her in the face and say "I'm all cut up, too." And he wants her to believe him because it's the truth—or, at least, it's what feels true to him. But she is too far

73

gone, and he wasn't even strong enough when he was seventeen to save himself. How could he possibly save her?

Franchise

A YOUNG GRANDMOTHER, still in her early sixties, sits with a mystery novel on her lap and watches her two grand-daughters and grandson play in the sun at Wyandotte County Lake Park in Kansas City, Kansas. This is her grandkids' favorite playground. It's a safe enough park, surely, but there are tough stories about this part of the city. The young grandmother feels safer farther south in Johnson County where the houses are bigger, and the streets brighter. It's not because those are whiter neighborhoods—at least she doesn't think that's the reason. She read a book last month on privilege and intrinsic prejudice, and maybe she just has all that.

Out of nowhere, Hayley Blue appears—nine years old with braided pigtails that stick cockeyed out of her head. She sits next to the grandmother on the bench while herds of children chirp back and forth on the multi-colored playground equipment.

The young grandmother turns to the unexpected child who is seated next to her and says hello. Hayley Blue (as she does) launches into a tirade about dinosaurs. Her favorite movie, as the young grandmother learns, is a tie between all the movies in the Jurassic Park franchise.

"You must want to be a scientist," says the young grandmother. "I read the book by Michael Crichton a long time ago.

It's full of science and math."

"No, I enjoy the parts where dinosaurs eat people," says Hayley Blue. "Like that one guy who is the hunter. He's going to shoot a velociraptor with his rifle, but then, boom, a velociraptor appears right beside him. The hunter whispers 'clever girl' because he knows the dinosaurs outsmarted him. And then: Down the hatch. Sayonara."

"They ate him?"

"Everything but his cowboy hat."

"Are you sure your parents want you watching the Jurassic Park movies? They seem pretty scary."

"My mom lets me watch whatever I want. Except Youtube."

To the right, three children wave frantically from a spinning wire cage—some kind of new age merry-go-round. She waves back, and then turns to the girl sitting next to her.

"Don't you want to play, honey? My grandkids are over there. I'm sure they'd play with you."

"I guess so."

Hayley Blue hops down from the bench and starts to walk toward the playground equipment. She pivots, though, after ten feet and stares right at the young grandmother. "I lied to you just now," she says. "I'm not supposed to like the parts of the movie where people get eaten. My cousin explained to me how weird that is. But I do like when T-rex wins. He's the hero of the movies. Like when he bit that stupid lawyer in half on the toilet. Or, in the new movie, when that rich guy sells all the dinosaurs, and you think for a minute that he is going to get away, but here comes T-rex—the real good guy—and he gobbles the rich man up at the last second. I guess that's still me liking the parts where people get eaten. But I don't want to be weird. I just like that T-rex always wins. T-rex winning is my favorite part."

Across the playground, a child screams. The young grandmother blinks and scans the complex, uncertain whose child made the noise, or whether or not the kid is hurt or playing. When she looks back, a tragic expression has overcome Hayley Blue's face. She doesn't know why, but she nods and says to the child in a slow, measured voice, "I know exactly what you mean."

White Landscaping Rocks

HERE'S A STORY OF LOUIE AND HEATH, who love each other. White landscaping rocks. Pampas grass. Is this a secret code? There's more: Purple decorations in the yard. A black ring worn on the right hand. Pineapple doorknockers. Even ridiculous garden gnomes. "You swing, right?" the neighbor woman across the way had asked one Friday. Heath had been getting the mail. "We would welcome a male couple with open arms," the woman had said, and Heath had stared at her.

In those first six months after moving to Lionsgate housing community (where everyone is beautiful), both Heath and Louie lost weight. Every sidewalk in the neighborhood was a fashion runway. Heath, who had never before exercised, took up jogging. Louie, who was most comfortable at home in sweat pants and v-neck t-shirts, donned form-fitting jogging pants and moisture-wicking tops, and silk pajamas at bedtime. They jettisoned their Friday night pitchers of Boulevard and mozzarella sticks for kale salads and mango smoothies. French press coffee from single origin beans. Heath even went through Louie's search history on the laptop and found that his partner had been browsing plastic surgery sites. What could he possibly be considering? A tummy tuck? A new nose? Absurd fake calves?

Slowly but surely the neighborhood ate them. And Louie and Heath fed on the idea of being eaten. "Look how those pricks painted their front door," Heath finds himself saying. "This will certainly come up at HOA," Louie says in response. The words sound ridiculous when they come out of their mouths, but the tone feels true. Yes, they find when talking it over; they actually want to say these words aloud. The two often sit in Adirondack chairs at the base of the driveway and sip Diet Coke, sometimes wine. They give Dan a thumbs up---the man in way-too-good-of-shape for his age mowing his lawn next door, shirtless and tanned to match the beige painted houses around him. Louie and Heath whisper to each other when Cindy Hawkins---pregnant for the third time in three years---floats past their property pushing a double stroller and talking on her Bluetooth. "There goes Fertility Barbie," they say.

At first Louie and Heath like their new bodies. They admire their tighter physiques and tell each other their asses look like a million dollars. They make love. They have sex. They fuck. They think about all the beautiful people in close proximity. All those lovely bodies crashing into each other. Before long, the world closes in. Before long, Lionsgate is the center of the universe.

And then, after a while, the physicality slows. Heath admits to himself that Louie might look better with a new stomach, or a stronger jaw, or a new nose. They can afford it, couldn't they? Perhaps they could "get work done" together. One could play caretaker while the other recovered. The strong one could hold the weak one's hand. Tell the other person how great they are going to look---how great the touching will be. Heath feels terrible for wanting to will the idea into existence.

This story doesn't have an ending. It doesn't have the balloon of Louie and Heath's relationship slowly leaking into a soft flatness. No intense Pop! that ends life as they know it. What it has is Louie talking more and more with the neighbor woman from across the way. They stand at the mailbox, laughing. They touch each other on the forearm when the conversation ends. And a few days later, Heath waves the neighbor woman from across the way over to Louie's empty Adirondack chair (because Louie is at a work thing), and Heath doesn't like to drink Diet Coke alone. Summer is ending soon. The days are getting shorter. Neither Heath nor Louie know what will come in the next week or month or year. But they both fear they are talking to the neighbor woman from across the way for the same reason.

There, There

OVERHEAD, THE SKY IS A QUILT of gray clouds. Tiffany drives down Highway 71. The sight of another vehicle on the road is rare, but each pair of headlights shining through the windshield reminds her other lives are out there, continuing on despite everything. The DJ on the radio—Chrissy Candelight of Mix 100.3—advises listeners to store vehicles in the garage tonight because severe storms are in the forecast. She wants everybody in the city to stay safe in their houses, to continue following the governor's orders to "please shelter in place," and to also enjoy this next hit from Journey.

The zoo, like the rest of the county, is closed. Tiffany can't shake the feeling that she needs to cry. Or maybe yell at the top of her lungs. The sensation is alongside her face—the same spot her boyfriend had slapped her less than two hours ago.

"God, that's not who I am," he had said afterwards, his voice breaking. "Tiff, please. You know me. That's not me."

The sensation feels like an oncoming sneeze that never arrives, or an unreachable itch inside of her mouth.

In an auxiliary parking lot, far from the zoo's main entrance, Tiffany kills the ignition. The spring air feels good when she steps out into the wind. It cools her face and makes whirlpools of her dusty blond hair. Instead of heading toward the empty welcome center and unmanned ticket booth, she walks a half mile or so around the fenced perimeter. After several hundred yards, the steel bars become chain-links. And then the chain-links become thick brambles and tree trunks. She cuts through the woods, officially trespassing. At first, she descends and tiptoes along the banks of a muddy stream before pushing her way uphill through thorns and vegetation. By the time she emerges inside zoo grounds, her forearms are decorated with pink scratches and her tennis shoes are caked with burrs and grime.

A dozen kangaroos, hunched in a field of yellow grass, watch her stumble out of the brush. She takes a step forward, and the kangaroos bounce away, their long, muscular tails curved at attention.

On the main concourse, the penguin exhibit is nestled between the polar bear cave and stingray tank. When Tiffany arrives, most of the penguins are inside. Sheltering in place, she thinks.

The heavy double doors are locked, but a few smaller penguins waddle outside by a shallow pool surrounded by an iron fence. The birds can swim through a tunnel and go in and out of the building as they please. Inside is a fake igloo atop a fake iceberg and a small, red-carpeted amphitheater. She remembers visiting the zoo on her fourth-grade field trip. The zookeeper had terrible acne and a little metal bucket of stinky, dead fish. Her classmates had squealed and pointed each time a bird dove into the chilly water.

A solitary penguin, the fattest of the lot, wobbles to the fence and stands next to Tiffany.

"Hello, beautiful," she says.

The penguin's black beak opens and closes, revealing a flash of orange tongue. The beak opens a second time.

"I'm sorry," she says. "I don't have any fish."

The penguin shakes its pelt. Thirty seconds pass, perhaps a minute. Its eyes stay locked on the girl's face. Rummaging through her jeans, she pulls out a pack of Trident gum. The penguin begins to chirp or chitter—she can't decide what to call the noise.

"It's not food," she says, popping a piece into her mouth and chewing. The penguin grows louder and more excited (or is it irritated?).

Worried that she will draw the attention of an essential

staff member—there must be security guards or zookeepers still working (what would she even say to them?)—she drops a piece of gum over the fence. The penguin gobbles the green rectangle and immediately begs for more.

"You'll get sick."

The penguin squawks, a piercing, desperate noise. The sound it makes, in a way, resembles exactly how Tiffany feels. Her hand, without thinking, moves to her face. She glances over her shoulder and scans the promenade.

"Okay, beautiful, but please be quiet," she says, and drops five more sticks over the fence. The bird eats as if it hasn't been fed in days. The rest of the penguins, like props, stand mutely in the background.

Tiffany sits on the cold concrete. A wind gust blows hair across her face, and she bristles at the falling temperature. The clouds are still light over the horizon, though, so she has more time. Perhaps a few hours.

The penguin doesn't sit but turns its plump body toward her. It likes her, she thinks, or maybe it just likes eating gum.

Slowly, she reaches through the iron bars. Her fingers halfway through, she hesitates. But then her hand moves forward until her palm rests gently on the penguin's wing. Its feathers are slick, an almost oily feel.

"There," she says. "There."

The penguin stares at her hand the entire time, but it doesn't move.

3.

My Neighbor, Ray

ON DAY THREE OF THE GLOBAL CRISIS, a person crawls out of my mouth. The person is small at first—the size of a marble—but then he grows and grows until full sized. It's Luke, standing in my living room, and he's free in the new world. An important thing to know: My name is also Luke.

Outside, Ray, my neighbor, hunches with his arms draped over the fence. Ray gazes across the Brookfield Housing Edition with its homes painted the color of rainclouds. Everybody wears sad eyes nowadays—from sleeping on sad pillows in sad beds. Luke appears.

"Ray," Luke says.

"I might lose my job if whatever company I work at gets hit too hard," says Ray. "I could lose my house."

"No, shut up, listen," Luke says.

"Do you think I could live in your basement?"

"Look," Luke says. "This is important. I'm trying to find something. And I remember that one time you were mowing the lawn and you took your shirt off. Remember that, Ray? It was over 90 degrees. And your headphones came out of your phone when you were bending to pick up the soccer ball the kids kicked over the fence. I could hear the music you were listening to. It was Pink Floyd, Ray. You can't put things past me. You know what I'm looking for."

"My mother would never survive if she got sick. She's a

heavy smoker."

"I don't have much time to be standing here," Luke says.

"God, you're funny," says Ray.

"I think you're funny to," Luke says. "But in a different way."

I'm staring from the couch. Luke comes back through the door, kicking his frustrations out on the rug. He doesn't have any choice, so he sits next to me.

"What happened to you?" he says.

"I don't know what you mean."

"You know," Luke says.

And I do know, but I don't feel the need to answer him. Not today, anyway.

"I think you should get back inside my mouth," I say.

A rustling beneath us. The white cat pops her head from under the couch. An instant later she tiptoes across Luke's lap, purring. The white cat does this thing where she sticks her nose up, begging to be scratched under the chin. Luke scratches just the right spot, and I can tell how much she loves him already. All at once, she is his cat and no longer mine.

* * *

The sun is a fireball blasting through the morning haze. Ten-thirty A.M. and already eighty degrees. I'm drinking coffee on the back deck, next to the gas grill. Below, on either side of the fence, Luke and Ray are having an animated conversation. Luke is laughing, head thrown back. At one point, Ray holds two hands in front of his chest as if simulating giant breasts. Everybody likes Ray more than Luke, which is fine, but then I am reminded that Luke only exists because he came out of my mouth, and then I don't know what to think.

"What?" I say when I feel eyes on me from below.

Luke says, "We're thinking about taking you for a walk today."

"I'm not a dog."

"You need out of the house," he says.

"I just left yesterday. Remember all those groceries you ate? I bought those," I say.

"Look at me. I'm outside."

"I can see that."

"Do you see what I'm doing? I'm talking to Ray."

"I can see that you're talking to Ray."

"Can you really?"

"You know I can."

"Here's a man who lives next door to you in the world," Luke says. "His name is Ray."

Ray takes a step back from the fence. He's holding a giant tube wrapped in wax paper. It's one of those gas station type burritos, and he's chewing with his mouth open.

"You don't know anything about Ray," I say.

"I know that Ray likes dance parties," Luke says. "I bet you didn't know that. He was a DJ once, in high school. Glam Rock. Disco Revival. He owned all kinds of sound equipment, and his hair used to be out to here. And this is the best part. Tell him your middle name, Ray."

"It's Danger," says Ray, his mouth full of burrito.

Luke raises his arms and nods in approval. He couldn't be more pleased.

"Congratulations on your new friend," I say.

"It's Maddie's birthday today," Luke says. "I saw it on Facebook this morning. You didn't write anything on her wall. What kind of friend are you? Not even interacting in the fake world."

"Actually, my middle name is Charles," says Ray.

"They don't call it a wall anymore," I say.

"What do they call it?"

"I don't know."

"And who is they?"

"They is people."

"People tend to behave like they're alive," Luke says. "Did you ever consider that?"

Not knowing how to respond, I shake my head and say, "I think you're full of shit."

I dump the rest of my coffee. The auburn liquid puddles and leaks through the slats of the deck, dripping on the kids' sandbox. Luke has on my sunglasses—the nice ones my wife bought me for Christmas but am afraid to wear for fear of losing them. He looks better in them than I do.

* * *

Unable to sleep, I reach for my phone and check the clock. It's 11: 02. The next time I look it's 11:04. And then 11:05. And I promise that's the last time. But the next thing I know I'm reading the numbers again, and they say 11:07.

I slide out of bed and venture into the dark house. Down the hallway, I see the kitchen light on. The sound of quiet voices talking.

Ray and Luke are sitting at the dining table drinking glasses of Jameson Irish whiskey on the rocks—a bottle that my dad gave me for Father's Day last year. The bottle rests between them, half-empty.

"Hey," says Luke.

"Hey," I say. "What is Ray doing here?"

"He lives here now."

"We've created a pod," Ray says. "I'm thinking about inviting my friend Johnny to join. And that woman on the other side of the street who goes jogging all the time."

"But you have your own house," I say. "We're supposed to be sheltering in place. Remember?"

"Do you think anybody gives a fuck about sheltering in place," Luke says. (He's had too much to drink.)

"The pod, though," says Ray. "That makes it okay. It's just like a bigger shelter, right?"

"You mean a bigger place?"

"What?"

"Never mind," I say.

"We can still get takeout," Luke says. "How in the world is that sheltering in place?"

"You won't know I'm here," says Ray. "I'll sleep in the

basement on the blow-up mattress. Litter box duty every day. And I'll play Xbox with your kids. I'll even go home to use the bathroom. My closets are full of toilet paper."

Too tired to argue, I crack a beer and sit at the head of the table between them. "Whatever," I say. "Just don't bother me when I'm trying to work."

"Anyway," Luke says. "I was telling Ray about this story I wrote in high school."

"Pretend I'm not here," I say.

"So as I was saying: This sixteen year old kid (about my age at the time of writing this story) had just gotten his driver's license, and he was driving toward Saylorville Lake, when all at once the entire world turned orange."

"Like the color orange?" says Ray.

"I don't remember this story," I say.

"Will you shut up and let me talk?" says Luke. "It wasn't like everything turned orange as much as it was all this kid could see was orange. No differentiation of objects, lines or shades. No start or finish. Just pure, constant orange in every direction."

"Sounds like a neurological condition," says Ray.

"This kid doesn't want to crash, so he pulls over to the side of the road, or what he thinks is the side of the road, and he climbs out of his car. He's stumbling in the orange fog, trying to get back to Polk City. Totally confused. Orange blind, I called it. He is walking with his hands out, and before he knows it, water is hitting him in the face. Somehow he's fallen into Saylorville Lake. And then he's swimming like crazy, attempting to find the shore. Everywhere is orange, and, through the panic, he's trying his hardest not to drown in the orangeness. Finally, after what seems a forever-long-swim, he gets swept into something hard. And then, bam. The orange disappears. The kid looks up. Guess what. He's in the middle of the lake, and he's pressed against the giant concrete abutments of the Mile Long Bridge."

"Is that it?" I say.

"No," Luke says. "He pulls himself together after a few minutes and swims back to his car. We're talking one drenched and freaked out kid. Resilient, sure, but exhausted and terrified.

And then, later, back at his mom's house, he sees a bag of navel oranges in the pantry. He takes the bag to the back patio and throws the oranges into the lawn, one by one. When they hit the grass, they don't make a sound. They just disappear into the night."

"I'd do the exact same thing," Ray says. He takes a long drink of his whiskey.

"That ending is terrible," I say.

"It's my story," says Luke. "I can end it any way I want."

"I'd love an orange right now," says Ray.

* * *

Ray stands in my backyard with his arms out. He's wearing a ridiculous red cowboy hat (that belongs to my wife). My three kids and Luke are treating Ray as a human maypole, except for instead of colored streamers, they are using toilet paper from Ray's closet.

The kids and Luke circle Ray, each holding a strand of the soft white line. The toddler participates for one lap, and then his toilet paper breaks, so he chucks the roll aside and continues on without it. Round and round kids and Luke go, covering everything below the red cowboy hat. Ray's stomach, his legs, his chest, his nose, chin, and forehead. The oldest kid works on Ray's arms. The middle kid does his ankles. Luke continually wraps Ray's neck until I hear a voice yell, "Jesus, that will do." They cover his mouth last, leaving an open strip for his eyes.

When they are finished, Ray resembles a crude mummy from the Wild West—or like a country music loving monk dressed in flowing robes. His body is one and a half times its normal width. All in the yard are pleased. There are at least a hundred stray strands of toilet paper caught in the fence between my property and Ray's.

Ray says something, his voice muffled. And then he says the same thing louder and staggers forward with arms outstretched—the creature re-animated. My kids run screaming into the windy afternoon.

For dinner, I'm making chicken tacos again. Everybody agrees that I make tacos too often—especially now. Nobody else volunteers to cook.

Ray, Luke and I are playing a game called "Mash Up" where we try to force together album names in a funny or interesting way. The rule is that both albums in the mash up have to come from the same band. Last round, I offered "Rubber Peppers Lonely Hearts Club Band." Neither Luke nor Ray thought it was especially clever.

Ray says, "Led Zeppelin 5."

I turn from the pan of shredded chicken and say, "There is no Led Zeppelin 5."

"Sure," says Ray. "Led Zeppelin II plus Led Zeppelin III."

"Or Led Zeppelin I plus Led Zeppelin IV," says Luke.

As if offering an alternative explanation, Ray says, "Heavy metal was an important part of my life."

"Metal was fun for about five minutes," says Luke, "when I was thirteen."

"Can you imagine a world without metal?" says Ray. "Not just the type of music, but a world without actual metal. How would we even function?"

"Jesus Christ," I say.

Ray leans back in his chair, arms crossed. "Okay, so here we are in the ultimate moment of what-if, and you won't even consider what-if? Fun conversationalists you all turned out to be."

Nobody says anything for a few minutes. The taco meat sizzles, so I add more tap water and seasoning.

Luke says, "Born this Monster."

"What? Springsteen?"

"No," says Luke. "It's Lady Gaga."

Ray begins to laugh.

"Look at you," says Luke. "Living in 1960."

"I wasn't even born in 1960."

"You could have fooled me."

Luke pushes Ray in the shoulder, and Ray pushes him back. My wife told me that over the last week Luke and Ray have become bros. They've filled the already-full house with their testosterone and bro-ness. The need for connection and human contact is strong, my wife said, and it has caught both of them, like kittens, by the scruff of their necks.

"Let's do songs next," says Ray. "The song 'Moby Dick' can mash with almost anything."

"There are other bands besides Led Zeppelin," I say.

"Just try it," Ray says.

I know what he's getting at, so I stir the chicken and say, "I'm not seven years old."

"No, no, no," Ray says. "Whole Lotta Dick."

"Trampled Under Dick," Luke says.

"Stairway to Dick," says Ray.

"Good Times, Bad Dick," says Luke.

Both attempt to list more Led Zeppelin mash ups but instead giggle uncontrollably. Ray plants his face on the table, the veins bulging like thin worms out of his pink forehead. Luke has to drink a glass of water to calm down. From the basement, I hear my wife and children yelling at each other. They are playing Halo on Xbox, or maybe Minecraft.

"I hope you like peppers," I say. "I'm going for it." Nobody seems to care that I am cooking all the meals. They never say thank you. The tacos appear in front of them, and they eat.

* * *

Luke decides that Ray should re-caulk the kitchen and bathrooms, and re-stain the cabinets. Ray is handy and doesn't mind, and he morphs into the happy worker bee on a Sunday afternoon—ever meticulous with his finger as he smooths the caulk in what can only be described as the perfect bead of white between countertop and wall.

"This stuff said clear on the tube," Luke says. "Why is it coming out white?"

"Probably it will dry clear," says Ray.

"That's impossible," Luke says. He turns to me—I am drinking a homemade latte—and says, "Don't you think that's impossible?"

"The tube said clear. That's why I bought it," I say.

"It's a major failure in manufacturing," says Luke. "Not that we've had any experiences with major manufacturing fails in this country."

Ignoring them, I return to my laptop and scroll through the writing prompts offered in the Facebook messenger chat windows. One prompt is to write a love poem between two inanimate objects. Somebody in the chat follows up by saying: "What is it with poets? It's always inanimate objects and how they feel."

"Hey, Ray," I say. My neighbor doesn't look up from his caulking. "What if I told you two inanimate objects could love each other?"

"They can't."

"But say they could. Say my razor and my toothbrush had feelings. Something like that. What would they care about?"

"Your razor would be jealous," Luke says. "Because you put the toothbrush's head in your mouth. All you do with the razor is slide it over your skin."

"You know," says Ray. "The most intimate thing you can do with a lover is touch their eyeball with your tongue. Very popular in Japan."

"But I'm talking inanimate objects, Ray. I'm asking your opinion on this."

He sets his caulk gun on the counter and wipes at a spot with a paper towel. "Well," he says. "Take the scenario between your toothbrush and razor. They sit together in the same holder, day in and day out. Leaning against each other. Both slowly wearing out. Both's purpose in life is to remove things from your body. They share your DNA, your daily routine. I could see the razor becoming jealous after a while, being as Luke said the toothbrush gets to go inside your mouth and the razor doesn't. But then again, every few months you throw the toothbrush away and replace it with a new one. The razor must feel lucky in its permanence."

"I replace my razor, too."

"No, you don't," says Ray. "You have a Gillette Mach 3 Turbo. You only replace the heads on those."

"I guess we're all sharing bathrooms now."

"Relax already. I borrowed one acid reducer pill. But now that you mention the razor's heads being replaced, I'd say the razor is jealousy-free for a week or so. You can't beat a razor with new blades. Gets the job done like nothing else. And if the toothbrush is looking worn and frayed, the razor has no problems in the world."

"Maybe, too, it forgets the jealousy when its brain gets replaced with a new one," I say.

Ray thinks on it a bit and says, "Maybe, but I doubt it. Just because an object has feelings doesn't necessarily mean it has a brain."

"There's no way in hell you've licked someone's eyeball," says Luke.

"Swear to God," says Ray, picking up the caulk gun. "My first wife. It was the sexiest thing I've ever done."

* * *

A cargo plane flies over the Brookfield Housing Edition. It drops leaflets, like giant snowflakes, over the eighty-some houses that make up our neighborhood. The leaflets spin together, dancing mid-air, before floating to earth. My unmowed grass is covered. My kids, ignoring my pleas, run outside to pick up the sheets of paper. They somersault and sprint around the paper-strewn yard. The front door explodes with their return, giving a leaflet to each person in the house and keeping one for their own.

"It's giant fortune cookies," my kids say. "You have to read yours out loud."

"And then, at the end, you say 'between the sheets,'" says a voice. It's Ray, my neighbor-turned-pod-mate, coming out of the hallway bathroom. No one is excited to see him, but here he is—part of our story.

92

Luke is fast asleep on the couch, snoring softly. The children put a leaflet on top of him. The white cat is curled up by Luke's feet, also asleep.

"Don't worry. It's not a good fortune," says the oldest kid. "It says 'Love a wicked witch today.'"

"Mine is weird like that one," says the middle child. "It says 'Don't stop when the group says stop.'"

"Better than mine," says the oldest. "Bad is normal. And normal is bad."

The toddler holds up his leaflet proudly. It says 40% off of a small blizzard at Dairy Queen.

The leaflet the kids give my wife says, "You are going to drink anyway. Might as well start now." She crumples the sheet of paper and throws it at me. Then she shrugs and goes to the fridge for a beer.

"Here, Dad." The middle kid hands me a leaflet.

My leaflet is longer. It's a full page about how men used to be hunter/gatherers, and how they used to provide for their family. How men today are afraid to take a fish off the hook—people like me are worried the fish will shudder and turn its fins into knives—or how we could never clean a fish, even if we have hungry mouths at home. Or when somebody rings the doorbell at three in the morning, and we crawl down the hallway toward the front door with a ridiculous golf club in one hand, shaking uncontrollably in a locked house. What are we going to do, drive the home invader into the fairway? Don't we know killers never ring the doorbell? People like me plant heirloom tomatoes, but we don't realize they come in yellow varieties. And the tomatoes grow beautifully and stay perfect for so long, but we never pick them. We wait for them to turn red like regular tomatoes, and then one day we wake up and find the vine full of yellow, shriveled corpses.

"Let's see here," says Ray. "This one says, 'The global crisis is going to take your life.'"

The older kids snort, trying not to laugh. But then they giggle uncontrollably. The toddler joins—always wanting to be included. Ray stares down the hallway, clearly bothered.

"Boys," I say. "That's not funny."

"The plane started it," the middle kid says, and that makes them laugh harder. The middle kid is doubled over now. My wife is sitting at the kitchen table, drinking one of my IPAs. She is glancing out the window, trying not to smile. Ray looks near tears.

From the couch, Luke springs to life. His uncut hair is wild—like the unmowed grass outside. He picks up the leaflet sitting on his lap and reads it. Holds it closer to his face and reads it again.

"What in the hell is this?" he says.

"Fortunes dropped from the sky," says the oldest kid.

"Somebody trade me," says Luke.

Everybody turns to Ray who is staring at his own leaflet. He looks up.

Hold Your Soul

THE CHILDREN of Mr. Lambert's first grade class each have their hair dyed a different color. It's expressivism, said Lambert to the parents at orientation, but the truth is the shades of hair help him keep the youngsters apart. He's seven months from full pension now—too tired to put another fifteen names with fifteen faces—and he longs to stay at home with his partner, who he leaves each day reading a laptop in bed, already blissfully retired and at peace.

During recess, the children are untethered and loud as hell. Lambert's kids are easy to spot—heads of pinks, greens, purples, and blues. They flame across the blacktop and stumble through the pea gravel, open-mouthed and slick-haired, their necks often stained with dye. Their feet pound up the twisty-slide ladder, and their knees bowl over any kindergartener baby too slow to get out of the way. Over by the basketball hoop, Yellow is being yelled at by Mrs. Sorenson. Neon Blue, who picks her boogers, has red streaks on her sleeves from this morning's bloody nose. Hot Pink has taken off his shoes again, for probably the fifteenth time today.

Silver, smaller than the rest, comes up to Lambert and says, "What is it and where do you put it?"

"What is what, dear?"

"A soul. What is it and where do you put it?"

Lambert doesn't answer.

"I was on the jungle gym," she continues, "and Tanner said my soul fell out and shattered on the ground."

"I see," says Lambert.

The little girl is crestfallen. She feels her limbs and face, and says, "Do I look different? Can a person be healthy without a soul?"

"You look the same."

"But how will I get my soul back?"

"How do you know there is such a thing as a soul?"

"Because there has to be something left over after I die. I can't just be gone."

Lambert studies her closely. He thinks of his partner, back in their apartment, drinking a latte and probably watching without him the Netflix show they were supposed to watch together this weekend. Lambert says, "You know, I think that was my soul. I hung it on the jungle gym many years ago with a piece of thread. The thread probably snapped after all this time, and I bet that's what Tanner saw. I wish I could have seen it explode, though. I bet it was brilliant. A person's soul should always go out in a blaze of glory. Or at least be left in a busy place, so there's always something to do and see. Under the jungle gym might be a good enough spot. What do you think?"

The girl considers for a moment. She nods and says, "I think you better not die before you get another soul."

Rubber Horsey Heads

APRIL 26TH AND THINGS BEGAN to get bad, bad. Two men in folding chairs, wearing rubber horse masks, sat and played accordions in the parking lot. They didn't want money, but several passersby dropped change into a discarded box that was sitting close to the men in horse masks. Some people thought it a joke. Smart ones kept their distance.

The first feral cat could have been an anomaly. Out my window, I watched an orange tabby with fur missing on one hind leg slink around the green dumpster by the old freight house and present itself to the horse heads. The cat stood in front of the musicians for what seemed a small eternity, back bunched like the silhouettes my kids and I hang from the ceiling at Halloween. And then the cat lowered its head. I hesitate to say the cat bowed—even now—because it wasn't exactly a bow. But there was something unnatural about it. Intentional.

More cats appeared from the alley. Out of the storm drains. Emerging between the tires of parked cars. Five or six black ones. A gray. One Siamese. Two pure white. One Tom so dirty, a walking dust bunny. The cats stood in front of the horse heads, arching their backs, and then ducking in submission. Soon the handful of cats became a small army. Hundreds. Cats everywhere, bowing to the horse heads. Congregating atop the curb stops, benches, and parked cars. Two perched on each arm of the fire hydrant. One straddling the one-way sign at the edge

97

of the lot. All the while, the horse heads continued to play their accordions.

I called for my children to come see this strange gathering. That's when the first cat presented a gift. I think it was a dead mouse. The cat dropped it on the pavement in front of the horse heads. A small orb of blood and fur. And then, the next cats offered their gifts. Song birds. Voles. A pigeon. A garter snake. Squirrels, their tails torn off. Chipmunks. Mice. Rats. A pile of dead things grew in front of the horse heads. By the end, it was three or four feet high.

A big ugly cat, missing an ear, came forward. The cat had something in its jaws, long and pink. It strode past the pile of corpses and placed the trophy at the feet of the horse heads. Then it climbed onto the lap of the left one.

I pressed against the glass of my window, trying to tell what it was. It could have been a weasel. Even a small, hairless dog. It looked, more than anything, like a person's forearm.
One of the horse heads stopped playing. He patted the ugly, one-eared cat in his lap, and then the horse snout turned toward my window. By the time I noticed he was staring, the one-eared cat was also staring. Soon the entire herd of feral cats had their necks craned and eyes fixed on my bedroom window.

My lights were off. The sun was out. If I didn't move, they couldn't see me. I told myself that over and over.

In Memoriam

"THE FIRST THING YOU NEED TO KNOW when you are driving to the airport from God knows where is that the surface area of this fucking town will absolutely eat you alive," she says. "And another thing is that once you get out of the city, some of the passengers will want to stop at a gas station to buy beer or liquor. But you can't do that in this state. You can play slot machines at the 7-11, but get yourself a drink? Not happening."

I met Lily at the downtown Oklahoma City YMCA. She was purposefully quirky, pierced twice in the nose, and purple-haired. She said that she liked my tiger-striped leggings, and after chatting for fifteen minutes on the stair stepper, offered to teach me how to drive a LYFT or Uber. She made decent money working nights and weekends. But, she said, you should always carry pepper spray. Or even something stronger if you have the stomach.

And, now, here we are (Lily and I), driving through the heart of Oklahoma's capital, heading toward a neighborhood called Bricktown. I had only been here a couple weeks. I don't know why I wanted to settle in this city as opposed to Norman where I would be starting classes in a few short months. I suppose, having never lived in anything other than what can be described as a small town, this could be my chance to experience something important—something metropolitan. So I rented a studio apartment with all the money I had saved over the last seven years. But soon I would be broke again, and I needed a way to make cash without trying too hard, or without reporting to a boss. That's where Lily came in.

"What's the tall one called," I ask pointing out the windshield at the bluish skyscraper that doubled the height of every other building in the skyline.

"I don't know its name. Some company," Lily says. "Make something up. The so and so center. The tower of the plains. Be creative."

"Will people ask?"

"Probably not," she says. "Think about it. Everybody in this city-full-of-fat-people has a car. The people who order Lyfts are either drunk or from out of state. And the people from out of state only have one point of reference to this shithole town."

"I don't know what you mean."

"Yes, you do."

"The only thing I've heard of is that one building that was blown up by the bombing guy."

Lily doesn't say anything for a few minutes, but I can see her glancing out the driver-side window. We are coming up on something that looks like a granite wall facing a manmade reflecting pool. On the other side of the pool, trees and markers that stand chest-high. She slows the car to a stop. It takes me a second to figure out what it is.

"Perfect timing," I say.

"I hate this thing," she says. "It's like everybody wanting you to show them the stump after your hand gets cut off." After a while I say, "Sorry. I should have been more sensitive. I'm not from here."

"Don't be sorry," she says. "All drivers need to know where this is."

Acai Bowl

HERE'S WHAT I'VE LEARNED: All suburban white women like pumpkin spice lattes between the months of September and November, and, when in Florida, something called an acai bowl.

The white woman I was with roped me into a food truck line that sold acai bowls so I could experience these purpley-frozen-smoothie-things. My students claimed I had the taste of *a basic white girl*. This woman wanted to know if they were right. Plus, she said, acai bowls are a superfood. People my age—36 years old—should be thinking about staying young as long as we can.

It wasn't really a date, but it wasn't really not-a-date.

Old people and alligators, I said to the white woman who wanted me to try the acai bowl. She had just asked me what I knew about Florida, and I was trying to be cute. She had lived in the sunshine state for three years and taught rhet/comp at the University of Tampa—a bigger school than I've ever dreamed of teaching at. I hoped she would invite me for a drink in her hotel bar after we attended the night's speaker, but I didn't want to set expectations.

Oh, yeah, I continued. And then there's that quarterback you all have. The one who became a meme for sucking on his fingers. He was giving a pregame speech or something.

Eat a W, the white girl behind us said. (She must have been listening the whole time.)

I nodded to the white girl in line and said, That's right.

The guy who ate the W. I mean, he ate his fingers. Or pretended to. My younger cousins showed me the video at Thanksgiving. We were playing touch football after the turkey, as we always do, and they kept yelling *Eat a W* every time they caught a pass or scored a touchdown.

I'd get a kick out of seeing you play football, the white woman said. (I don't know if she was flirting.)

When it was our turn, we ordered the acai bowls. I picked the regular, which came with bananas and granola. The food truck guy said they would take five or six minutes to make, so we found a close-by bench. Even though my watch showed after 5pm, I was sweating—overdressed in my long-sleeve button up and slacks. Thankfully, I hadn't worn a tie.

In the parking lot, there was a shirtless college-aged kid doing tricks on a skateboard. He had long, braided hair and one of those ultra-lean physiques that you can only have when you are younger. He wasn't X-Games good, but he was skilled enough to spin on two wheels, and to land little jumps and grinds on the concrete curb stops. After a while, I realized the white woman and I were both staring at him.

The skateboard kid came rolling over at one point, and I asked him what kind of board he had. I used to have a deck myself, back in the 90's, but the best I could do was mess around the driveway.

It's a Birdhouse, the skateboard kid said. (I pretended to know what that meant.)
The white woman smiled and said, I could watch you skate all day.

And when she said it, I was reminded of this time in college when a girl I had a crush on told me she was going to the rec center to see the soccer team practice because soccer players had fantastic legs, and she liked to watch them run.

I knew the woman sitting next to me was a completely different person than the girl from college. But I felt, in the moment, the same desperate urge I had to trade all my good attributes in for new ones.

Re-energized, the skateboard kid turned and glided away

from us. The sun was directly behind him. He spun and became a rotating silhouette.

Human Resources

GRETA WAS HIRED AS HR DIRECTOR on a Tuesday. We knew right away she was dead. Samantha screamed when Greta limped into the office, but she was the only one.

My life, to that point, resembled the GIF of suited people sitting around a boardroom table and then raising a fist and yelling "let's have a meeting!" at the same time. Seven or eight hours a day, meetings. Consider me checked out. Phone between my knees, scrolling through Twitter or commenting on my friends' Facebook statuses. Nobody cared if I was in the room.

Management didn't hide the fact that they'd employed a dead person. The new HR Director, they said, was vetted, qualified, and stamped as approved. Anyone who took issue with the hire could look elsewhere for work.

One cold day, the new HR Director stood at the window alongside Fantasy Football Travis and his Grumpy Cat mug.

Greta, as always, drank nothing.

"Do you see that man down there in the Kansas City Chiefs coat," she said. "He is a bad man."

"He's okay," said Fantasy Football Travis.

"He paid teenage girls seven hundred dollars and gave them a video camera," said Greta. "They needed money. He knew it."

The man outside, a maintenance worker, was spreading ice melt in the parking lot. All at once, he dropped the bucket and grabbed for his throat. One hand reached to the sky, fingers kinked. The other hand pulled the skin at the front of his neck.

Soon, his head was as red as his coat. We watched the man spin, crimson-faced, and then fall to the pavement. We stared.

Greta turned and said, "Guys, I didn't have anything to do with that."

The meetings continued. Every day. Monotony. Infinity. Greta, always present, preferred to sit in the corner of the room, facing the wall. She wore dresses that resembled nightgowns. Some found her attractive. When she wanted, she could move quickly and appear without warning. Typing at your desk, and she'd materialize on the cubicle divider, sitting cross-legged and staring down like a crow perched in a tree. During the afternoon huddle, I watched her leave her chair and slither along the carpet, a giant, human snake with fanned hair. Momentarily, she disappeared under the conference table. Then her head slowly rose between my knees. I was reading on my lap a Buzzfeed article about affairs people have had with their personal trainers. After a few seconds, she nodded for me to scroll down. When I obliged she looked up and smiled with dead, cracked lips.

* * *

Soon February arrived, and with it our annual performance reviews. Tyler, the HR Director's office assistant, knocked on Greta's door and said her 11:30 had arrived. I was the 11:30.

"Close the door behind you, Tyler," said Greta.

I touched his arm and said, "You're welcome to stay."

Tyler gave a big, fake laugh as he left and said, "You two need time to gab."

Greta stared at me for a long time. Then she said, "I didn't kill Sammy." I realized I had placed my hand, without thinking, over my throat.

Removing my hand, I said, "Who is Sammy?"

"From Maintenance."

I said, "You've been going through my desk at night. Each morning, all the drawers are an inch open."

"So what?" she said, shrugging. Her nightgown nearly slipped off her shoulders with the shrug. She smelled faintly of cucumbers, not like death at all. I understood why people found her attractive. Hair the color of coal, wideset eyes and lips, porcelain skin. I wished for a second that her dress did fall. But she was dead.

"Today was my birthday," she said.

"How old are you?"

"I don't remember."

"Well, happy birthday. I hope it's a good year."

She looked away from me and said, "It's also the day that Veronica died."

"You aren't allowed to know that," I said.

Her words were completely out of bounds. I never talked about my sister, not with anybody.

"It's in your file. You took two months off of work."

"I don't care," I said, raising my voice. "Veronica is off limits. I have work life and I have life life. Those two are mutually exclusive."

Our eyes met for a long time. She liked me, I could tell. Her normally sharp face had softened, and she seemed like she wanted to reach out and cup my cheeks. Instead, she opened a manila folder on her desk and slid a sheet of paper toward me.

"You've had an adequate year," she said.

"Are we getting a COLA?"

"What do you think?"

"Whatever," I said. "Will you stop going through my desk, please? It makes me uncomfortable."

My phone rang. It was the George Harrison song "I've Got my Mind Set on You." I claimed that song years ago as my happy song, and made it, for a short while, my ringtone. But I always kept my phone on silent, and my current ringtone was set to cricket chirp.

"You're getting a call," she said.

George Harrison started up again. Embarrassed, I fumbled through my coat pockets, trying to hit mute. And then it dawned on me. I didn't have to read the caller ID. I knew what the name was going to say.

Normally, I'd go cold. Goosebumps. Chills. Nerves unwinding. All the pain and grief and what ifs. Waterfalls on top of waterfalls. Grinding me down and drowning me where I sat. But my reaction was muted—unexpected. A dull combination or resignation and anger. I shook my head and said in a quiet voice, "Why would you do that?"

Greta looked heartbroken. "I think you should answer the phone."

"I don't want to."

"Please," she said. "Please."

Wendy's Eclipse Day

IT'S ECLIPSE DAY in Missouri, 2017, and it's about to start raining. Wendy, the niece, is sprinting out of the Lost Lake hiking trails and into the parking lot that overlooks the spillway. Above her is the grassy, Smithville dam, several hundred feet high, and in front is the campground in which is gathered about three or four hundred Smithville reidents sitting in lawn chairs, anxious to see one of nature's most discussed spectacles.

But the sun. Wendy is looking upwards in her paper eclipse glasses. It's 90-some percent covered, and the clouds are moving in. The clouds. The I-can't-believe-this-is-fucking-real-life clouds. God is sick. God is joking. All day, blue skies, and now. Two minutes to go. Two minutes to totality. The sun is swallowed.

Wendy keeps running past the playground and into the field. There are dumbshit campers about, sitting outside their dumbshit RVs and Winnebagoes. Somewhere behind is her aunt and her cousin. But that doesn't matter. They don't matter. If she runs fast enough, she could find a break in the sky. She can still see it.

The light around her dims. The clouds are starting to win. But that's not correct. Totality is beginning. Wendy is frantic. She throws her glasses into the grass and opens her iPhone. She can film it, maybe—two minutes and eighteen seconds of night in the middle of the afternoon.

Concentrate, she tells herself. Listen for the sound of locusts. The nocturnal animals will awaken.

But then, the crash and screech of fireworks. The campers and people in town. Every Thursday, Friday, and Saturday night of the summer they do this. But now—it's a free play. Two minutes and eighteen seconds of new firework time. Two minutes and eighteen seconds to light every fuse they can before the clock runs out on the sudden and miraculous darkness.

Wendy is only fourteen years old. Her life has lasted fourteen trips around the sun. But she could kill everybody in the world.

TIME Magazine Person of the Year

IMAGINE A CLASSROOM tucked away in the corn and bean fields of Middle America. Outside the sliding window, a windy fall day with brown and orange leaves still clinging to their perches. In the distance, yellow cornstalks with drooped ears. The history teacher at the front of the room is young, just two years out of college. She wears her hair in a ponytail and gestures to a projected image on the front board. She says, "Look at this list. In 1937, Chiang Kai-shek and his wife Soong Mei-ling were declared TIME Magazine's Person of the Year, followed by Adolf Hitler in 38, Josef Stalin in 39, Winston Churchill in 40, Franklin Roosevelt in 41, and then Stalin again in 1942. Can anybody tell me what that shows us?" The students in front of her, mostly sophomores, don't respond to the question. They stare at the wall behind her. When she moves back and forth along the front of the desk-line, their eyes move everywhere she is not.

There is one boy in the middle of the pack wearing a denim shirt. His name is Aaron, and he tracks her every movement. The history teacher has gathered over the last two months that this boy, Aaron, is in love with her. He holds on her every word, as if each joke or quip she makes about turn of the century America might be singularly his. Every day, when the bell rings and students explode out of their seats, Aaron stays behind and asks the history teacher questions, as if she is an old friend. "Did you watch that new horror film about the priest who murders people in the confessional?" Aaron wants to know. "I'm looking to buy some new jeans. Have you seen any sales?" he asks. "What's your take on guys with short hair?"

The history teacher searches the faces for eye contact, anybody but Aaron. One of her strengths is her ability to ask questions and let the silence linger. She can wait her students out, and they are always the first to flinch. After forty-five seconds, Natalie in the corner raises her hand and says, "It means the world was messed up then. Most of those people are terrible."

"But then leaders emerged," says Aaron, turning in his seat. "Great leaders because of it."

"I agree with Natalie," says Dawn, from the front. "Aaron is wrong. This whole list is full of terrible men. Mostly white and Christian. It should be called TIME magazine's Evil-White-Christian Man of the Year."

"So you're seeing a pattern, Dawn?" the history teacher asks.

"Unquestionably," says Dawn.

The history teacher is about to challenge the assertion, but the bell chimes, breaking the spell, and the room fills with laughter and disrupted furniture as the students make their way to seventh hour. Aaron is slow to leave. He fills his backpack without looking up or asking one of his obnoxious questions.

"Have a good day, Aaron," she says.

He turns to her. For a moment, she thinks he is going to cry, and then he says, "I'm going to go out and live my best self."

She doesn't know what that means, but when she pats his arm as he walks by he looks at her as if she is his last hope.

Karate Witch Teacher Kickass

THE GAUNTLET IS THROWN. Go time serious path of destruction. Garrett—who is the worst person in the world—wants to fight Jalen. And it's for real. Not in some sanctioned karate tournament like Daniel Larusso. Not outside a bar with an audience pressed against the windows. No boards and padded helmets. No punches thrown at a mirrored wall. Real blows. Pain in the forefront. One v one. Four legs enter. Two walk away.

Location: to be determined.

Time: when the sun screams.

Deep down, the excitement builds in Jalen's stomach. All that talk about self-defense was one thing. Self-preservation. Self-care. The larger tapestry of the self. But where's the fire? Who carries the beef? Garrett is made of beef. The beef is here and now, and definitely on fire. Jalen doesn't care about the beef, and yet the beef exists. It's calling out to be real, to be a thing, to be had, and Jalen is the type of person who will have it. Garrett. What a shithead name. A cosmic joke ready to be told. Six pounds of shit stuffed into a five-pound sack. A million pounds of shit stuffed into the sack of a bagworm. The little caterpillar inside drowning. Shit-deep. Garrett, up shit creek, calling out to Jalen as he is swept away. "It's on like Donkey Kong," Garrett says, splashing in shit-water. Like anybody could get behind that old school lingo. 1993 is calling on the rotary telephone. 1993 is twisting the loopy cord through its fingers and smoking a cigarette in front of its children. In the background, must-see-TGIF-television plays. On a rooftop party, Jaleel White is showing Laura how to "Do the

112

Urkel." The kids are drinking Crystal Pepsi and playing Hungry Hungry Hippos on the shag carpet. The point is: 1993 is calling, and it wants its sense of humor back.

When Jalen agrees to the fight, Sensai Majo's older brother whispers "hell to the yes" and pumps his fist as if this is the best news he's heard in years. He stares at his plump, clenched knuckles which are turning the slightest shade of pink.

* * *

Jalen, twenty-eight years old, jump-kicks and cracks a board. The students—karate kids— many of them half or a third his age, burst into applause. Crazy awesome fantastic. Sensai Majo holds the two pieces of board in her hands. Unbelievably unimpressed. She's maybe remembering when she cracked her first board—how she didn't make a big deal of it. When they met, Jalen had asked if she was from Japan. "I'm from Kansas City," she had said, prompting him to say, "God, I'm sorry."

Beautiful sexy ageless. Sensai Majo is Sensai Witch. She moves as water moves. The hardest stomach imaginable. Nothing like her stocky, rager brother who teaches classes on punching and blocking, and who likes the dollar menu at Taco Bell. "Jesus H Christ," Jalen had said when he found out. He and the rager brother were in the drive-thru line at Taco Bell, ordering spicy chicken quesadillas and having laughs. "What kind of witch? Broomsticks and cauldrons. Or does she talk to trees?"

Some evidence existed. Most specifically Sensai Majo's soft spot for crystals. Jalen fell once, twisting his ankle during a spar, and the next thing he knew the beautiful instructor was kneeling next to him and rubbing a blue celestite over his foot. She hummed in a hushed tone. Then she pressed the crystal against his forehead, right above his nose. "Get up and finish," she said.

Another time, he passed the dojo's office and she was seated at the desk, pretzel style, massaging her thighs with a green stone, so brightly colored it nearly glowed. That's when his crush for her started. He remembers thinking how he wanted to be made of stone. How he wanted to be rubbed up and down her

113

legs.

The rager brother, his mouth full of spicy chicken que-
sadilla, said, "She allows things to happen in the universe. You
know Alice with the hick accent? My sister broke seven of her
co-worker's fingers. Some dude who steamrolled Alice in front
of the managers. Seven fingers like saltines crackers. Snap, snap,
snap, snap, snap, snap, snap." The brother rapped on the dash-
board each time he said "snap."

Jalen stopped laughing. He drank a swallow of Sprite and
said, "I don't believe you."

* * *

Raymond, another math teacher, is a person Jalen dislikes. Not as much as he dislikes Garrett—who is the worst person in the world—but enough. Raymond is six and a half feet tall
and sits at the round table in the faculty lounge. He's eating "hot
lunch," which teachers only do when they forget to bring their
own food. Today is chicken patty on bun day, with bright yellow
corn and crinkle-cut fries. For dessert, a snickerdoodle, which
Raymond eats first. His mouth full of cookie, he says, "You've got
to be shitting me, Jalen. What's with the gloves?"
Jalen glances down at the ninja-style fingerless gloves on his
hands. He says, "They're from Dick's."

"That figures gloves like that would come from a place
called Dick's. I'm playing, though."

In his gloved hands, Jalen holds a too-the-brim black
coffee and a half-finished protein shake. Next to the two math
teachers sits Jana, the PE teacher, and Courtney, who teaches science. Courtney is a regionally-ranked triathlete. Jana, described
by the students as "country strong," founded the local chapter
of Crossfit. Jalen enjoys sitting with these women—the three
of them athletes—and hearing their discussions about why the
Kansas City Chiefs will never win back-to-back Superbowls.

Courtney takes a long drink of milk and says, "Those are
decent lifting gloves, J."

"They're over the top," says Raymond.

Jalen crosses his arms, hiding a glove in each armpit. It does look silly, the jet-black polyester clashing with his faded slacks and cheap tie.

"You're making him self-conscious," says Jana.

"I'd want to know if I looked that over the top," says Raymond. "Wouldn't anybody?"

"You're negative," says Jana.

"It's realness. I'm sorry for being real. That's me."

Jalen forces a smile and says, "How's the team looking this year, Ray?"

Because no one else volunteers, Raymond is in charge of the boys' high school basketball team. The district only cares about football, track, and especially girls' basketball—which wins the state title season after season. The boys' team is an afterthought, generally finishing last or dead last in the conference. It's common knowledge that the only thing Raymond coaches his players on is slam dunking and alley-oops. Raymond, at six foot six inches tall, can easily dunk, and he believes dunking is the ultimate flex—in life and in basketball. He leans back in his chair and rubs his chin, as if thinking. He says, "Oh, you know. We're decent. Two of the starters can ball. Maybe a third with proper coaching, and if he hits the weights this semester."

Jalen examines his fellow math teacher, as an opponent this time. A towering lanky figure with eyes a bit too together. A shaved, doughy head with thick eyebrows constantly wedged in a V. Pendulum arms with good reach and strength but no quickness. Deer-like legs that could easily tangle, or topple with a hard sweep. Raymond, always the biggest person in the room, has no idea how to defend himself. He is nothing like Garrett—the worst person in the world—who Jalen has agreed to fight at month's end.

* * *

Sensai Majo watches from her office while her rager, older brother teaches the class the "money punch." There's a punch one can do, but one shouldn't do, that stops time. It's the rogue

115

wave that wipes out the stupid surfers on the beach with their dumb, salty hair and ridiculous board shorts. It's the cheat code. The downburst. The atom bomb. The trick is, of course, that one has to get to a place one doesn't want to go in order to summon the money punch. A place that lets evil deep inside one's core. A pinprick opens in the heart flesh, and black slime trickles in. When mixed with droplets of slime, the blood of the heart turns dark red, but, soon, the red is overwhelmed and the heart is entirely black. It's a water balloon, expanding with slime. And then the slime is out of the heart, swelling the veins and arteries from a hundred tiny cracks. Spilling into the outer body. One is no longer sixty percent made of water. One is composed entirely of compromised organs and slime. The slime is alive and fully charged, swamping the mouth and eyeballs so that when mouth and eyeballs open, there is slime and nothing else. One is no longer recognizably human. A slime monster, animated. One is The Blob, but un-freezable this time and trapped in a human husk. Guided by slime, the limbs spring forward in terrible ways and with the strength of ancient energy. Jalen can tell that the rager brother is teaching this lesson expressly to him. He wants Jalen to use the money punch on Garrett—who is the worst person in the world.

"It's not money punch," Sensai Majo says. She is out of her lair, dark hair flowing every which way. Her piercing eyes as serious as Jalen has seen them. "It's called the leaf punch."

She stands barefoot in front of Jalen and the rest of the karate kids in the way she does with palms thrust downward below her black belt, knuckles kinked. She continues, "The leaf punch is never to be used. It's an uncontrollable attack."

Her brother snorts, but Sensai Majo doesn't flinch. One of the karate kids, a yellow belt, raises her hand and asks why it is called the leaf punch.

"Leaves wet by snow or ice," Sensai Majo says, "collapse an entire tree. Leaves brush your forehead before a giant bough splits open your face."

Nobody understands, but the karate kids nod in agreement.

The rager brother, as if to prove a point, walks toward the hanging punching bag on the far side of the room. He stalks around it, like a starved bear, circling. Brushing against it with his shoulder. Testing and loving on it. Then, finally, when it looks as if he has lost interest, he delivers a thunderous blow to the bag's center, which causes the chain to squeal as the canvas swings wildly.

Next to the spinning bag, which has become unhinged due to the force of the violent hit, the brother stands triumphant and panting. One of the karate kids behind Jalen says, "that was sick as hell" under her breath.

After a few seconds, the rager brother mashes his knees with his palms, bending and coughing. It is as if he has been sprinting. And then he is sitting there on the mat, wiping the sweat from his face with the sleeve of his gi.

"Money punch," he says in a quiet voice.

The students turn back to see what Sensai Majo has to say, but the front of the room is empty.

* * *

Jalen's students sit in front of their desks with crossed legs, those of them who are willing and able participants. A few stay in the chairs, bending their faces down and resting their foreheads against the enamel desktops. All eyes closed. Lights dimmed. Several of them hold hands. Jalen is cool with that, but he snaps his fingers at the couple in the back of the classroom who try to cuddle. He couldn't have been clearer: The last five minutes of trigonometry are for group meditation, not goofing around. On his phone, he plays crashing ocean surf (sometimes gentle rainforest) on maximum volume. It's a phone, though, so it doesn't sound great. The students get the message.

Jalen, after he is certain the students are in the right space of mind, begins to think, as he always does, of Sensai Majo. Lately, he has been imagining the story her brother told. The one where she broke the guy's seven fingers—the dude who works with Alice (with the hick accent). In his mind, she's waiting in

117

the parking lot. The dude is getting into some douchebag car like a Camaro, and there she is sitting in the passenger seat. He doesn't scream or cry out, because he's too soft-headed. He says, "Sweetheart, you scared the bejeezus out of me." And the dude thinks maybe this is going to be one of those meet-cutes like in a romantic comedy, or, better yet, the start of a really good erotic film. He thinks this while Sensai Majo takes his sweaty hands, lacing her slender fingers through his. And then, without warning, crunch.

Or, in the other scenario, Sensai Majo sits alone in her house, eyes closed and cross-legged on the hardwood floor. A candle sits before her. She's meditating like all his students are now. And then, somewhere on the other side of the city, the dude who works with Alice screams in agony. He's cradling his broken hands against his chest, and swinging his head back and forth, trying to determine the source of the pain.

Jalen opens his eyes. The couple that was trying to cuddle is now full-blown making out. He watches the two students paw at each other, their sloppy mouths coming together with equal parts shamelessness and desperation. Without thinking, he again snaps his fingers at them, six, seven times, until he commands their attention. The couple stops necking, but he isn't looking at them anymore. He's staring at his own hand. More specifically, the bones inside his skin. He's thinking about the noise he had just made.

* * *

On a Thursday night, Jalen sits in seiza before the long mirror—his knees and shins flat on the mat, buttocks resting on his heels. When he had first began studying karate, sitting this way caused intense pain, but now he can sit seiza for hours.

It's late. The dojo is empty, aside from Sensai Majo and her brother. She wears a black gi and stands like a ghost in the front of the room. Her rager brother practices front kicks against the newly remounted heavy bag in the far corner. The sound of his lungs heaving and bare feet slapping leather fill the room.

Jalen closes his eyes, trying to concentrate. After a minute, he feels the weight of someone kneeling on the mat. When he opens, Sensai Majo is sitting seiza next to him, also facing the mirror.

After what feels a long while, she says, "You've been a good student."

"You've been a good teacher."

"I know," she says.

From the corner, the rager brother grunts loudly and attacks the bag with a flurry of kicks and jabs, exhausting himself, until his punches are weak and sporadic.

Jalen says, "I don't want you to do anything to Garrett."

She glances over and says, "I'm not the one fighting."

"And you can't talk me out of it either. This is my life."

The sensai rubs her colorless fingernails up and down her thighs. He thinks she is going to laugh at him, chide him like a little boy. Instead, her eyes are serious. She stares into the mirror reflecting them and says, "When I was young, I found a woman who had escaped from a prison."

Jalen waits for her to continue. It takes a few minutes before she does. "There was a minimum-security facility by the stockyard," she says. "We lived in a small town outside the city. I don't know how she escaped. My brother and I were catching leopard frogs at the pond. She was hiding underneath the gazebo. I could see her through the lattice and cattails, crouched there in the dark.

"When the police showed up, they brought a dog with them, and the dog found her right away. They let the animal drag her out because she wouldn't crawl out on her own. She started to cry when they showed her the handcuffs. Each time she pulled her wrists away, one of the officers (another woman) hit her forearm with a baton. The prisoner was older, in her late sixties. When they were finished, she couldn't lift her arms."

"That's horrific."

"Yes," she says.

He exhales slowly, feeling the emptiness of the large room. "What made you remember this woman?"

"She's always there, in the back of my mind. The image of her under the gazebo. How she trembled and held one finger to her lips, and then folded her hands in prayer. She wasn't praying. She was begging me to protect her."

* * *

It snows overnight. An October snow. Only a couple inches, but it doesn't matter to the trees in the neighborhood. There is one big one, Jalen's favorite, on the walk between parking lot and high school. Sixty feet tall with a hyperbola trunk as wide as the picnic table that sits underneath it. Oval leaves the size of footballs. The chains from a nearby swing set twist and creak in the cold wind. Jalen walks from school to car, as he does every day, scarf knotted in the neck of his pea coat. He isn't tough enough for this dramatic change. Not after so many warm afternoons in the beginning of the month.

A sophomore is filming with her smartphone next to the tree. He thinks he recognizes her from trigonometry. She has one hand on the trunk. The other holds the camera at eye level.

With the snow's weight and the wind strain, the leaf stalks are coming undone. It's raining in Missouri. Spitting little flecks of snow and ice. Or, more accurately, there's sleet in the air, and the sky is full of falling leaves, swirling and tumbling through the atmosphere.

Jalen steps past the sophomore, who is engrossed in the scene surrounding her. A few paces later, he turns to see her spinning in the middle of the dropping leaves, arms spread and head back, unaware that anyone is watching. Above, the wind continues to strip the color off the giant tree, still proudly green this late in the year. The outsized leaves are unable to hold on. Unable to settle to earth. It's beautiful and oddly unbearable to look at.

The end of October has arrived so fast, he realizes. The tree isn't ready. He wonders if Garrett, the worst person in the world, is ready for Sunday. Has Garrett been training as hard as he has?

120

Jalen has no idea what to expect.

*　*　*

For reasons unknown, Sensai Majo asks Jalen to meet her downtown. Is it a date? A lesson? A random act in a series of random acts that make up her existence? Her brother insists on driving Jalen to the venue—stopping at Taco Bell on the way, of course—and then, in the drive thru line, saying "never mind" to the kid who asks if he can take his order. The rager brother looks at Jalen then, the engine running, and says, "You don't know what tonight is about, do you?"

"I'm going to an escape room with your sister."

"That's a good mindset," says the brother. "I'll be outside if you need me."

It's Saturday. The night before the night. The sun is nearly down when they roll into the parking lot. The place is called Pop-A-Lock: Escape Rooms and More. Jalen shouldn't be stunned at the sight of Sensai Majo for the first time in regular clothes—leather jacket, tight jeans, a black tank, and violet bra straps on either side of her neck—but he is. Perfume, lip gloss, and hair spray. Crazy sexy mysterious. All at once he feels out of his element and over his skis. Underneath his sweater, perspiration gathers in his armpits, and his mouth turns dry. He kicks himself for not eating a handful of mints before he left, for not spritzing himself head to toe with his Nautica body spray.

Sensai Majo barely acknowledges him or her rager brother, other than a curl of the finger that means follow her inside. Jalen closes the truck door and thanks the brother, who watches intently, a grim expression on his face. Jalen hopes his friend will drive away, but he doesn't seem to be going anywhere.

They are already late for the seven 'o clock orientation. Jalen, having never participated in an escape room before, cringes at the thirty-bucks-a-person cover. In the lobby, some dude with curly hair is explaining the rules to a small gathering of people. "It's all in good fun," Curly Hair is saying. "Work as a team. Think simple. Reverse engineer the puzzles. All that stuff you watch on Youtube."

He leads Jalen, Sensai Majo, and four other strangers into a room deeper inside the building. Overhead, there's a large clock that reads 1:00:00. One of the walls is plexiglass, one is sheet rock, one is jail cell, and one is brick. Each wall contains a door. There are three different desks, a chalkboard, and a scattering of books on the floor. Pieces of paper are taped, at random, to surfaces. They could be clues, or false effects placed to throw off the players.

"Is everybody ready?" Curly Hair says. "Oh, and the record for this room is 39 minutes."

"Ready for what," Jalen says, looking directly at Sensai Majo. She doesn't answer.

* * *

The next thirty minutes are confusing. The four strangers, who all must know each other, get to work on examining every nook and cranny of the room, every drawer, every slip of paper. Clearly, this isn't their first rodeo. The fifteen-by-fifteen-foot space is full of motion and noise. The strangers jabber to each other, saying things like "There's a sequence of five letters. Everybody keep your eyes peeled for anything with five letters." Sensai Majo sits atop one of the desks while Jalen circles the room's perimeter, attempting to be helpful but not really part of the team. He doesn't know the rules of the game, only that they are trying to open one of the doors. All exits appear locked. He tugs each handle, just to be sure. There's a theme or story, supposedly, something they are trying to solve, but the basic idea is straightforward: Get out of the room before the clock hits zero.

Eventually, after several laps, he sits on the desk next to his sensei. She doesn't seem bored. Disinterested might be a better way to describe her.

From the other side of the room, the players whoop. They've unearthed a key they announce—not to a door but to a lock box that contains a clue, though none of them know what it means.

"Good work," Jalen says. And then he jumps off the desk and says, "Shit-fuck-shit-fuck-shit."

Three feet from where he is sitting, on the other side of the jail wall, there is a strange man with wild hair pressed against the bars. The man's face is splattered with blood. He's wearing an explosive device on his chest—a vest covered with wires and square packets. The man laughs in a high-pitched cackle, causing all heads to snap to attention.

"You have twenty-three minutes to live," the man tells them. "In twenty-two minutes and fifty-six seconds my little darling goes off and we all become pink mist."

The man crows with more ridiculous laughter, throwing his head back and yanking on the bars with his hands. Hamming it up. The four players on the other side of the room ignore him, already hard at work on the next puzzle. Jalen recognizes the man. It's Curly Hair from the lobby, wearing mascara and a wig. The blood on his face is probably catsup.

He bends his head toward Sensai Majo, hoping for some sort of guidance or understanding of what she wants from him, but her face remains a blank slate. This is stupid, he realizes. A cheap-ass establishment that makes their staff double as doorperson and actor. A waste of thirty bucks and a perfectly good Saturday. He steps away from the prison wall and rips at the door of the brick barrier. It won't budge. Hopelessly locked. He could bust out, maybe. He's seen Sensai Majo's brother shatter bricks many times. He would yell "Kiai" and then there would be a fist and red dust where the brick once was. Jalen could do that, in theory. Punch through the wall and unlock the room from the other side.

He feels a hand on his sleeve, pulling hard against his forearm. Twisting him like a rag doll. He spins and meets Sensai Majo—powerful dreamlike strong—inches from her face.

"Listen to me," she says in a voice no louder than a whisper. "When the door opens, your enemy is going to walk through."

"I don't have any enemies."

"Listen to me," she repeats. "What are you going to do

when your enemy walks through the door?"

"When the door opens, I'm getting out of here."

"Don't play games with me."

"But this is a game."

Her eyes burn a hole in his forehead. "Tell me what you are going to do when your enemy walks through the door."

He doesn't know why, but he says, "I'm going to fight."

"Who are you going to fight?"

"My enemy."

"And who is your enemy?"

"My enemy is Garrett."

"That's not right. Who is your enemy?"

"I told you. My enemy is Garrett."

"That's not right," she says again.

She kisses him, hard. On the lips. He can't believe it. He's swimming. And then it's over.

He says, "My enemy is whoever walks through the door."

"And what do we do to enemies?"

"We fight."

"Good," she says. "Whoever walks through the door. We fight them together."

"Okay," says Jalen.

"Together," she says.

Behind the bars, Curly Hair screams. "Sixteen minutes! In sixteen minutes, we all die. No one escapes the final sleep!"

But there isn't sixteen minutes left. The game is nearly over. Cheering by the chalkboard. The four other players have found the final key. They are celebrating and slapping high fives. All that is left is to figure out which of the doors the key will open: sheetrock, prison, brick, or plexiglass.

The sheetrock is no good. The glass door has no keyhole. The jail door is padlocked, but opening it would let a crazy man with a bomb inside their room, so that can only mean the key belongs to the brick door. Final puzzle piece held aloft, the four players walk triumphantly toward the exit.

"Kokutsu-dachi," says Sensai Majo.

At her command, Jalen assumes the defensive back

stance—left foot forward, trailing foot at a forty-five degree angle. Next to him, his teacher falls into the more complicated stance of neko-ashi-dachi.

He looks to her, and she looks back. They both face the door.

4.

Ball Pit

YOU AND I HAVE TRAVELED back in time, friends. It's Showbiz Pizza in the late 1980's. Richard Marx plays over the house speakers. Denim shirts and neon, neon, neon. On stage, Billy Bob the mechanical bear is on the fritz. In a roached-out, striped apron, he laughs hysterically in a robotic squeal. One eye hangs from a spring, bouncing and swaying next to his bear snout.

From all angles and directions, arcade games pulsate MIDI sounds. We absorb the music into our skin. I stand behind you, left hand on your shoulder, right fingers splayed between the circular buttons and ball-on-a-stick controller of player two. Your ninja character, dressed in blue, is surrounded by foes. One by one you cut them down, and then you flip-jump from a higher rooftop toward a lower balcony. But you short the jump, and your ninja falls to his doom. The screen fades. A countdown appears, from ten. The bad guys have our hero strapped to a table in some backwoods shed. Behind him, they stand in a semi-circle, mouths agape in wicked smiles. Each passing second, a spinning circular saw descends through the middle of the screen. "Continue?" the game urges. We are both out of quarters. You look at me and say, "Fuck." The word is drowned out in the electronic din, but it exists in the three feet between your lips and my ears. Later, you pull me by the sleeve into the monstrous ball pit. The epicenter of the night. Inside the nets, a turf war rages. Colorful orbs flying in every direction. Soft and weightless as dinner rolls. Nothing hurts in here. We give ourselves to the pit in terrible ways and always survive.

Your face emerges from the kaleidoscope—a talking, severed head. "There's a dead girl at the bottom," you say. "I dare you to swim down and kiss her eyelids."

Your grin is wide, and there are gaps between three of your teeth. I don't believe you, but I like your smile. I will follow a born liar anywhere. We both dive into the depths of the pit, tunneling our way downward through the multi-colored balls. Underneath, it is warm and difficult to breathe. We must be ten feet down. Maybe 100.

You reach the bottom of the pit before I do. The dead girl is there, as you promised, but she isn't a child. More a woman. A dead woman with long, stringy hair and gray skin, and she's holding you against her body as if you are her baby. Between so many colorful circles, you are frozen in time. I am also stuck. Unable to go deeper, unable to pull you away. How can I see you, I wonder, in the darkness? How can the light reach through so many layers? How long can we last down there, in the bottom of the pit?

Afterwards, we sit at the long table, eating pizza. I keep staring at you. Unflappable and unfazed. No pizza touches your lips, but you drink an entire pitcher of soda.

"Rashad," I say. "Why won't you eat anything?"

You tell me you've never been thirstier in your life. When you say it, your voice sounds like the voice of someone pretending to be you.

Puffy Man

MYDAUGHTER LAILAH FEARS the Jackal Man more than the Puffy Man, but the Puffy Man is no picnic. Puffy Man hangs around the forty-five-pound-and-up plates at Muscle Beach on the south side of Venice with his crew of Puff People. Puffy Man is by far the puffiest. My daughter makes sure to point out this distinction to my son, who just turned eight.

I walk the sand with my two children on Thursday evenings. That's our time to spend together, and Venice Beach is where they like to come when the moon is up and the tiki torches are lit. We hold hands often, because in a way they miss being around me—and I miss being their everyday dad. But then, when we get close to a place where things make sense, here comes the Jackal Man in his horrible, wooden mask and filthy clothes. He seems to be always waiting for my children around the next palm tree, or springing forth from the blanket-nest of homeless people who sleep in huddles near the ocean.

It's a bigger city than any of us are used to. The three of us miss the openness of Missouri. Sitting down to dinner. Gas stations the size of small mansions. Thunderstorms and gravel roads and deciduous leaves.

Our beach isn't always scary, though. There was that one sundown when I ran all three of us, fully clothed, into the water. My children had seen the ocean from the car, but all of us had yet to go in. I remember the first waves nearly knocking Lailah down, and then there was my son, pretending to be tough but squealing when the Pacific cold hit him in the face. I laughed the whole time, struggling to hold onto my kids' wrists against the ocean's strength.

Knee deep in saltwater, I looked over the pink Pacific and

spun in a slow circle, taking in the city around me. The sunset splashed our shadows across the shore. Our outlines mixed with the other spectators on the beach, all fixated on the overplayed miracle of the West Coast sundown.

In the background, one shadow was in motion. It was the Puffy Man—ever vigilant, doing his pullups in the last seconds of daylight.

Showdown

IF ALIENS HAD INVADED the planet when I was eight years old, and I was given a choice as to whom I would pick to champion Earth—the biggest and the baddest human on the planet against the biggest and baddest creature from outer space—I wouldn't have hesitated. I would have picked Mike Tyson. And in this scenario, Mike Tyson would have never gone on to do terrible things to women, or bite off another person's ear, or tattoo his face, or lose a child to a terrible accident. In this scenario, Mike Tyson would square off, bare-knuckled against some multi-armed-six-eyed-crustacean-slash-insectoid under the lights of Madison Square Garden, or Caesar's Palace in Vegas, or maybe the ruins of the Roman Coliseum in the middle of the night. And it wouldn't matter so much if you were from Des Moines, Iowa, or Damascus, or Leningrad, or Rio De Janeiro, or Hong Kong. The noise would be deafening, us screaming at our rabbit-eared televisions. "Save our flawed existence, Mike." Destroy this hideous creature who shadowboxes and taunts our shirtless champion with its gross-lobster-arms. Or maybe (my eight year old mind erases all that nonsense), there is no fanfare. We cut to Mike Tyson fighting this horrible-dripping-alien-fighter in the middle of the ocean on the back of a gigantic blue whale. And we don't get to watch, because this isn't our fight. The whale just floats there, hoping in its whale mind for a quick ending to the pain above him, and every so often a military dolphin flips itself onto the fighting surface, trying to take out the insectoid's legs—because, after all, this is their planet too. We aren't the only ones who live here.

Common

HE DIDN'T THINK IT WAS A BLESSING. It was what you didn't talk about, especially in the first twelve weeks, because it might happen, so you didn't say a word. Superstition sealed lips. It was common. That's what the book in the school library said. A spontaneous loss before the 20th week. A cause for distress, but not a lasting cause for concern. So common, in fact, that it wouldn't be sad, not like the sadness left when a real life ends.

Beasley had done his part when it happened. Pressed his lips against her forehead, held hands and said the Lord's Prayer. It's only a light going out. Blood on the morning sheets. Not meant to be. A fire spark, flashing momentarily, and then fading against brick. It wasn't a person. It didn't have a name.

If they loved each other enough, they didn't need friends. They didn't need family. Before it happened, they spent whole days kissing, and nights whispering into the glow of their cell phones. He wore her favorite necklace looped three times around his ankle, hidden beneath the left sock. She taped his basketball picture next to her pillow. They promised to remember their first kiss each time the clock read 9:47. Months passed like minutes. They were dating, then boyfriend and girlfriend, then in love. He loved the way she could pin her hair in place with a pencil, the way she sipped a carton of orange juice as if she wanted nothing in the world more. He loved the way the muscles in her legs stretched away from volleyball shorts, and he loved the way she had once moved his hand from the clasp of her own hand to the clasp of her bra. Their love became physical. That's when Beasley learned a lesson on chance. Once is alright, once is safe, but seven times because he was too afraid to buy condoms---seven times might be enough to worry about. But making love was better without a condom. Making love didn't feel wrong if warmth touched warmth without partition.

This is a tired story. The first test came back plus sign, and the one after that, and the next one still. Beasley blamed himself, fate, his irresponsibility, his seventeen years of age. How could he have done this to her, the one he loves? How could he have done this to his mother? Hadn't she made the same mistake? Hadn't she shown him how difficult life was when you lived this way?

On the day the first thing happened---the making part---Beasley went jogging on the bike trail downhill from his mother's apartment. Along the creek bottom, where the trail turns north, he encountered a dead black snake, four feet in length, its carcass stretched limp across the left side of the asphalt. Half of the snake's body was covered in a tree's shade, the other half---the tail half---baked in sunlight. Beasley prodded the snake with his sneaker. There was a depression in its back, flat with striations. He flipped the carcass, revealing a soft, gray belly, a bit of blood. How many snakes passed over these trails in a given day? How many times had this particular snake gone back and forth before a bike tire finally caught it?

She was sitting on the porch when he returned from his run. They couldn't get inside fast enough. They made it halfway up the stairwell. The sweat dried on his skin before he stood, apologizing. He hadn't pulled away at the last minute like he'd planned. They hadn't been careful. That was his job, not hers.

When this common thing happens, it hurts. Not the way it hurts to hold a stillborn child in your arms, but it hurts in the way you hurt when the one you love doesn't love you as much as you love her. You put a part of yourself out there, into the unknown, and that part is taken. Maybe it's not as real as the part of a snake lost to sun and a bike tire's weight, but a part of you disappears nonetheless. A part of you is left on the trail, lifeless.

She says thank you to God when it happens. She says God gave us a second chance at happiness. She holds a plush rabbit on her lap, cradling it with both forearms. Beasley had picked the yellow rabbit at the store, because twelve weeks are not enough to know the right color. The one he loves' dark hair hangs long and loose. This is the first time Beasley sees her without makeup; the first time, too, he understands what she means when she says the happiest times are the quiet happy times. Is she happier now than she was at 9:47 all those months before when his lips found hers? This common thing, she tells him, is God's way of taking care. He watches as she pets the stuffed rabbit's pelt. She winds the rabbit's ears between her fingers.

Beasley thinks the worst part is not the thing that is gone. The worst part is that no one knows. It's common to keep quiet, especially this soon, so his mother never cries. She never returns a piece of folded clothing small enough to fit in the palm of her hand. Beasley tries to decide if he should cry. Is it reasonable? Appropriate? He wonders if the one he loves will keep the rabbit. Perhaps she thinks the rabbit was hers in the first place. Her mother and father probably cried when they found out. But will they cry when they learn what happened? More importantly: if you don't know a name, if you don't know a face, what do you imagine when you close your eyes?

Beasley hangs out with his boys after it happens. They raise hell in starlight. Another tired story. He gets stoned at a party. He drinks too much. He and his boys throw things off the balcony. Plates, old VCR tapes, pieces of glass. An empty bottle explodes against concrete, and Beasley wonders if that isn't him exploding. In the dark of his friend's bedroom, he kisses a girl, reaches a hand down the front of her jeans. She has a face. She has a name, but he doesn't know it. He can't remember if she kisses him first, back, or even at all. This is what Beasley wants to tell the one he loves: When it happens, something real dies, but it isn't inside of you. It's inside of me.

What happens is so common that the world moves on. Beasley spends afternoons working on his jump shot at the 95th street court. The one he loves sits in the paint-stripped bleachers, texting on her cell phone. If she hears the clang of the hoop's chain-link net, she looks up and says good shot. He clowns the celebration---his shooting arm raised, his fingers chasing the arc of the ball downward, the soles of his feet bouncing in cadence-

--but she isn't watching anymore. She used to pretend his long arms and quick smile could melt her knees, but that has changed. Everything changes. He isn't the same person who is taped to her bedroom wall next to the pillow, who made the clock stop at 9:47 months and months ago.

Beasley buys condoms, now. He is no longer afraid. It will never happen again, she tells him. For the rest of our lives, we'll be careful. But Beasley knows the times are numbered. They are already lost. Soon enough, the one he loves will consider a new path, and Beasley will find boredom in the nightly phone calls, the touch of her kiss. The thing that happened will really be just a thing that happened. And the thing itself will actually be gone, and over, and done with, and the saddest part will be that he isn't supposed to feel sad. Or maybe he really doesn't. Not anymore.

Miss America

THERE'S A LAW THAT SAYS you cannot hitchhike (or attempt to hitchhike) in the Missouri town of Mexico. Chapter 26, Article 18, Section A in the city code of ordinances. Roommates Gertie and Rosie decide to break this law on a Friday, because there is nothing else to do anyway.

Gertie and Rosie, sophomores at the University of Missouri, wear workout clothes—pricey yoga pants and Under Armour Mizzou Tiger tees—that way people looking to pick them up will recognize the irony of what they are doing rather than thinking these two are down on their luck. It will, Rosie figures, decrease the odds of them getting brutally murdered, because who would murder two college girls?

A boy from their dorm who always wears Led Zeppelin shirts drops the girls off at the downtown square of Mexico. The tiny city is not dead-dead but pretty-dead. A few cars here and there. Sad, old people shuffling about. Surrounding the block are rust and clay-colored brick fronts sporting faded awnings with crappy, chipped lettering. At the square's heart: a squatty government building made of newer, nicer bricks. The only thing of note is that every tree, bench, and light pole is adorned with a white, diamond-laden sign advertising the upcoming Miss Missouri competition. "Celebrating 50 Years in Mexico, Missouri!"

Gertie shows one of the signs her middle finger and snaps a selfie.

"Miss Missouri is a real thing," she says. "I can't believe it."

"Oh yeah. This girl I know from Southwest Village competes every year," says Rosie.

136

"That's gross."

"It's not so bad. Pageants are about feminism now. Empowerment. Diversity. It's about loving yourself. Not like the old days."

"That's horseshit. You're so 'Missouri.' There's nothing feminist about a beauty pageant."

"I don't want to argue."

Gertie smiles. "It's because you got high again last night, isn't it? That's why you are in a bad mood. You're ashamed you ate pot gummies with Kevin, and now you think Jesus isn't going to let you into heaven or something."

"You're not funny," says Rosie.

The two girls hike once around the square and consider trying a frappe at the local coffee shop. They decide they would rather go out to a late lunch when they get back to civilization. At this point, the time for talk is through, and so they plant themselves on a corner of the square that seems relatively "busy." Donning their best smiles, they stick their thumbs in the air—officially breaking the law.

A couple cars wave at them but nobody stops. Zero windows roll down. After a while, Gertie sits on the curb and scrolls through her phone. Rosie doesn't give up, though, and she continues to pace back and forth in front of the stop sign, thumb at the ready.

"God, look at this," says Gertie.

"What?"

"There was another school shooting today. Two people have died. Congress is already sending out thoughts and prayers."

"Where was it?"

"I don't know. I didn't click on the story."

Rosie says, "My heart hurts to think about that stuff."

Both girls are silent for several minutes. Rosie studies the sky and wishes it were a sunnier day. She hates the monotony of overcast clouds. How everybody seems bitter and impatient. Finally, she says, "We should have made a cardboard sign that says 'Columbia.' I bet people would give us a ride if they knew we had somewhere to be."

137

"We don't have anywhere to be."

"Maybe I do."

"Trust me. You don't. And I certainly don't."

"I have things going on," says Rosie. "I have someone waiting for me."

Gertie tilts her head back and is unresponsive for a few moments. Then she lowers her chin and says, "You could take off your pants. Like the Miss Missouri pageant is the feminist way to get a scholarship. Taking off your pants could be the feminist way to get a ride."

"I meant it when I said you're not funny."

Gertie says, "I know you did."

Red Line

WHEN HE WAS IN HIGH SCHOOL, he entered the red line station off Ontario Street. There's no good way to say this. He was going down to jump in front of the L-train.

Everything has a why, but there wasn't a why for this. He was tired of being ignored---that seems close enough to an answer. He wasn't beautiful. That played a part. And he is not an irrational person, but, in 2017, there was a hollowness about waiting for a message from somebody he cared about. Text me back. Email me back. Message me back. Refresh and repeat. His problems were more widespread than that, but tunnel vision took over. Even though he understood what was happening, he could do nothing to stop it. His life would go on if he didn't throw himself onto the tracks. He would do more things and meet more people, but that all seemed like somebody else's story. At seventeen, his heart felt ready to stop beating.

About fifteen seconds after he descended the stairs, a train went screaming by. He wasn't prepared to jump. Easily, he could have done it, but he got caught in his mind. He thought about whether or not it would hurt. Would he be dead before his body was able to process the pain?
The train he had missed was so fast---faster than he remembered them being.

A girl (about his age) in a yellow coat grabbed his wrist. She said, later, that he had this look on his face like he was about to do something terrible, and he kept talking to himself. He was leaning off the platform, trying to see down the tunnel for the next train light, and she thought he might fall. When she touched his arm, he turned from the tunnel. She shook her head and said, "Don't."

And that was enough to make him flinch. He started to say, "I have to. I have to do it," and he thought he was just talking, but it turns out he was yelling at the top of his lungs. The people on the platform surrounded him. He tried to break away, but a big man pinned him down. He pleaded and sobbed, but it was too late.

Here's more tunnel vision: The girl in the yellow coat had been the most important person in his life. And he was furious at her for not letting him jump.

Chicago, to the rest of America, is most lovable as a caricature. Old Style beer. Deep dish pizza. Go, Cubs, go. It's easy to forget that one hundred and fifty years ago this city was made almost entirely of wood. A summer with no rain. A barn on fire. Then a building, a street, a river, a downtown. A conflagration that nearly consumed all. Three hundred dead. Thousands of homes destroyed in a fire that future generations will describe as "great."

In the end, Chicago remained. Hard-nosed people emerged from the smoke and ash, ready to rebuild with steel and brick. Tough people---such as the big guy who pinned a seventeen year old kid to the cement or the girl in the yellow coat---patting a seventeen year old's useless, sobbing body with so many hands as if he were on fire. They weren't going to let him burn. Not in their city. They put him out. He didn't realize he wanted them to. But they knew.

Man Show

LATE FRIDAY NIGHT, Andy tells Cam to drive with him to West Des Moines. There's a nightclub called Kitty's or Cat's or Black Cat's or something like that. Andy assures him it is not a strip club.

"Fun people dance there," says Andy. "And they have a 'body contest' on the stage at midnight. The winner gets 100 bucks. Best shirtless dude. Best chick in a sports bra. Audience vote by loudness. I probably won't win. I don't have the definition, but I figured you couldn't lose."

"My body fat is all over the place this month," says Cam.

"No, man. You have this in the bag."

So the two gym rats enter the nightclub. Andy orders a whiskey and water, and dances with a cute girl in a summer dress. Cam eats a glass of ice cubes and has a twenty-minute conversation with the bouncer—nice dude. Funny stories. Great shoulders.

At 11:45, the body contest kicks off. Three women enter the female division. Only one looks to have ever worked out in her life. The other two are grossly overweight and, Cam thinks, have entered as a gag. The female contest quickly wraps. The athletic woman leaves the stage with a 100-dollar bill. The two heavier girls stumble back to the dance floor, howling with laughter.

Next, it's the man show. Cam and Andy stand bare-chested, shirts in hand, in a horizontal line with eight others. They are the only two men who spend any significant time in a fitness center, though a couple of the younger guys are naturally muscular. Two even show hints of abdominal definition.

Some asshole on stage (the host?) parades around the contestants. He asks them to turn around or flex. When Cam and Andy flex, they actually have something to show off. The other guys don't compare.

The asshole host says it's time to get serious and narrow things down to a top two. Cam is certain it will be him and Andy. Maybe they can give each other a nod and each take home fifty bucks, regardless of who wins. The asshole host showcases each dude, and eliminates the ones who don't get big cheers. Andy gets a raucous reception. The asshole host declares him one of the finalists.

Now it's Cam's turn. The host says, "Can I hear it for Adonis here? Do you think this guy works out?"

In the audience, one of the heavier female contestants from earlier yells, "His tits are bigger than mine."

There is no roar of approval or appreciation. People laugh instead at what the woman yelled. The asshole host prompts them a second time, and the response is no better.

"Sorry, brother," he says to Cam.

Cam puts his head down and steps back as Andy and one of the guys with a hint of abs step forward. It's not the end of the world to lose. Cam has lost at many things.

But, as the tilt-o-whirl of colored lights and amplified sound washes over him, he thinks maybe it is the end of the world.

Kingdom of Teeth and Scales

THEY LIVE AROUND US. Everywhere there is water or tall grass. Forest-green scales. A snout. An eyeball. A blast of warm breath. And then a mouthful of teeth coming at you. These creatures survived what all other dinosaurs could not. Through asteroid collision and epic forest fire and ice age. Through every volcano on the planet shooting its top six miles into the air. Pterodactyl bodies falling from the sky like wet leaves. Supine T-rexes spinning in the dirt with their strong legs, unable to get up with their pathetic, baby arms. Brontosauruses, their backs and tails on fire, munching stupidly on leaves—the sensation of burning not able to jump synapses between tail and brain fast enough to save a life. All else died, but the alligator lived on. From New Orleans to Baton Rouge—from Texas to Florida. Gatorworld USA. Kingdom of teeth and scales. The last of the terrible lizards.

People know you as the Cajun girl, though you are only half Cajun. You speak French, sometimes, but only do so when you've been drinking. People find that charming about you. Your thick bangs and eyes that sit just deep enough within your face to appear sad.

Late at night, you stand next to a wiry high school boy. He has platinum hair on his head and pretends not to be afraid of the silent creature at the edge of the water. The gator stares at you and your friends, lids unblinking. "Watch this," the high school boy says to the group. And he nods in your direction. He is a little bit cute and a little bit Family Circus. You might want to kiss him later, you think. But your thoughts are interrupted by the screaming.

The creature has the high school boy by the arm, pulling

him toward the river. For a moment, it looks like it is going to drag him back to its lair. But then the gator spins, and the high school boy falls backward. *The death roll.* You don't know why you recall its name, but you do.

In the backdrop, the creature fades into the dark water. The boy, in shock, is spread eagle on the ground. His left arm ends unnaturally in the weeds. A surreal swirl of green and red. The group surrounds him with hands on their faces.

Impossible Naked Life

GENEVIEVE COMES BACK TO LIFE, naked on the rocky ground. Sunlight peeks through the branches of the crude roof of her makeshift shelter. A man lies next to her, also nude, but she hardly knows him. There are no blankets. No coffee. No breakfast to be had of any kind. Nothing intimate happened last night except she and her partner had collapsed, exhausted, onto a bed of soft pine needles as they had done for the last six nights in their efforts to beat the ultimate test of survival on cable television. The campfire simmers outside of the makeshift wigwam—hopefully enough to keep bears and mountain lions at bay. A producer of the series, a tiny, commanding woman, assured Genevieve that she kept a high-powered rifle in the production trailer, and wasn't afraid to use it.

At first, it was one reality show about trying to stay alive in the wild without any clothes on, but then came renewed seasons and offshoots and reboots, and one became three became thirteen consecutive iterations, became fan threads and wikis, became a show after the show where a bald man and two women sat on a couch, sampling red wine and talking about what had happened in tonight's episode—who was being impossible, who was acting as a slave to instinct, and who was the model survivalist.

"See the thing is," the producer who owned the high-powered rifle had explained to Genevieve at the open casting call, "this can be your platform. Many contestants have jumped to another series after their episode. Some become regulars, fulltime actors even. And it's all very tasteful. Everything in the front is blurred. You don't need to worry about what your mom or dad is going to think."

145

"My parents are dead," Genevieve said. That wasn't really true.

"I'm sorry to hear that. I didn't know," the producer said, and she wrote something down in her notebook.

Groggy in the wigwam, Genevieve wonders, again, why they decided to pair her with a man instead of a woman. Barry, her sleeping partner, is ninety percent patchwork beard and love handles. He has terrible, British teeth, breath, and accent. His body odor fills the shelter. She can smell herself, too, the sourness of unwashed skin. No hygiene exists in this camp, though she could walk just over a mile and bathe in the ice-cold glacier stream if she wanted to expend the energy. Otherwise, no shaving, showering, or deodorant. Eventually, she read somewhere, their bodies will adjust and she and Barry will simply take on the scent of the mountain. Until then, like their nudity, the stench is something they must learn to endure.

Barry grunts and rolls to his back, exposing his sagging testicles and small penis. She can't remember his age—late thirties or early forties. Previous contestants on the show say they had gone the entire month without an erection, but Barry doesn't seem to be bothered by that particular affliction. On the first night, she spent hours staring at his genitals while he snored softly by the campfire. They were ugly to her, but also, at the same time, fascinating in their ugliness.

Without opening his eyes, he says, "I'll have ham and eggs, love. And a caramel macchiato with soy."

She examines her partner—fat, lazy, small penis and all—unsure if she hates him, or if she is just dirty and tired. She says, "We have edible roots and rainwater. But you have to dig them up yourself."

* * *

Two days ago, while gathering firewood, Genevieve heard Barry scream. The sound of a human voice piercing the mountain silence froze her blood. She sprinted toward camp, as well she could in bare feet—dully aware of her bouncing breasts and jiggling stomach, the stinging of rocks and sharp vegetation under her toes—but fear of her partner being fanged by a cougar or rattlesnake pressed her forward through the trees.

When she reached the clearing, her eyes watered from pain and anxiousness. There he was—her assigned, fat partner—yelling and hurling rocks at a pair of mountain cottontails. The rabbits were incensed, running in figure eights through their camp. Too frightened to escape in a straight line.

"Meat," he yelled at her.

Her stomach burned at the idea of food. Forty-eight hours had passed since they'd last eaten. One of the rabbits sped past her, a blur of ears and puff tail. Without thinking, she swung the hatchet at it, the blade not coming within five feet. Lack of nutrition and sleep had slowed her reflexes. Her arms were moving underwater, swinging through molasses. She chopped again, harder—on nerves alone—missing the rabbit by inches this time. The creature retreated toward Barry who roared and chucked more stones its way.

The circus ensued for several more minutes—rocks and hatchet flying—until the rabbits came to their senses and fled down the mountainside, leaving the two naked contestants gasping for breath at the edge of camp.

There were four camera-people assigned to this episode. Genevieve hardly noticed them anymore. One stood alongside. Another at the vista, framing the man and woman's silhouettes as they looked down the hill.

"That's right. You better run, you furry fucks," said Barry.

After Genevieve's breathing slowed, she said, "God, I'm so hungry."

"I've never been this hungry," said Barry.

She looked down. Bright blood streaked the bottom of her leg. Somehow, in the madness, she had nicked her shin with the hatchet.

Barry—a horticulturist in real life—had one good attribute, and that was his knowledge of plants. Within minutes, he had her cut washed and a handful of yarrow pressed against the wound. He set her down by the fire and gave her a drink.

"Take a load off for a few minutes," he said.

"Thanks a lot," she said. "But we have to do better than this. We'll never last the month."

"I know."

"I'm not going to quit. It's not an option for me. Do you understand?"

He patted her shoulder with a callused, dirty hand and said, "Love, you nearly split a hare."

She stared up at him and said, "That's really stupid." And then she laughed. She wasn't sure why she laughed. Maybe to make him feel better, or funnier, or more likeable. Perhaps she wanted him to know that they were still on the same team. Out of the corner of her eye, she could see one of the camera-people, tiptoeing closer and closer—lens trained on her face.

* * *

When Genevieve had seen the show in the past, she binge-watched it on her laptop under the dim lights of her bedroom. She ate Goldfish crackers and drank ginger ale with crushed ice, and marveled at how the contestants just laid there in the make-shift camps, starving their asses off. Why didn't they spend more time searching for food? After a while, when it became a real possibility that she would be a contestant on the show, she began to remove her clothes and watch. One night, she looked over at the full-length mirror next to her bed. Her slouched breasts pressed against the mound of her stomach. Her backside curved gently in the gap of the seat. She stood and examined herself from different angles and positions—amazed at what she looked like from directly behind and to the left, or from underneath, or in a military push-up position, or when she stood atop her chair and lifted one knee.

Now, living the show in the flesh, she understands. The

hunger takes over everything, including, even, the will to search for food. Dragging another log onto the fire takes all the energy she has, and she crumples again on the pine needles next to Barry.

"Alright," she says, exhaling. "I think I'm ready."

Barry places a bundle of yellow flowers and stems onto her stomach. Dandelions. The most common weed in North America—ubiquitous enough to grow even here. He had picked them this morning, and had already himself eaten close to a pound of the plants. Taking a fistful, she grimaces and then pushes the whole mess of yellow and green into her mouth. They are sour, and then bitter.

"That's it," says Barry. "Just a nice herbal salad. Crunch and down it goes."

She swallows hard and says, "I'm going to throw up."

"No, you're not. These are perfectly edible."

"Let's hike to the stream and try to catch a fish."

"I don't have the strength for that walk today."

Stuffing more dandelions into her mouth, she says, "You never have the strength."

Barry places another bundle of weeds onto her belly. Quietly, he says, "Eat a little more. We have weeks to go. This is a marathon, not a sprint."

"We can't survive on grass."

"Mountain Huckleberries grow wild in this region," says Barry. "They put blueberries to shame. Bite into one and it explodes. Tart and sweet at the same time. Imagine a big pile topping a bowl full of vanilla custard."

"Stop, please. I'm too hungry for food fantasies right now."

"Think, though. Warm biscuits with butter. French fries topped with gravy and cracked pepper. Homemade bread and honey, fresh from the oven. A pint of hard cider, ice cold."

Genevieve rolls and, with effort, rises to her feet. Dirt and pine needles stick to her legs and shoulder blades, her constantly sweating ass. She gathers two sharpened sticks from the wigwam and stands over the top of her horizontal partner.

"Where are you off to?"

"I'm going to take a bath because I almost smell as bad as you do," she says. "And I'm going to stab the biggest fish you've ever seen right through the heart."

* * *

The stream water is liquid ice, but she forces herself to squat in one of the deeper pools. With her palms, she scrubs her armpits, her vulva, the undersides of her breasts, and between her legs and the cheeks of her backside. She dunks her head in the water and emerges, gasping from the shock of cold. Barry would never subject himself to this, she realizes. He would continue to save his strength and stink up the camp for the rest of the month, oblivious to his own rancidity.

The entirety of her skin pebbles when she steps out of the stream. Warmth is nowhere to be found, no matter how much she rubs her flesh with her hands. Taking an outdoor bath is the first activity that actually made sense to be naked, but now she misses clothing more than ever. Hugging herself and shivering, she staggers alongside the stream, dripping and counting the seconds to dryness.

In a bend, maybe fifty yards down, she spots three shapes in the clear water. Her heart skips. All at once, cold is an afterthought. Mountain trout. She takes a few anxious steps closer, and the fish flee in a flash of bubbles.

She turns to the cameraperson following her and says, "They can see us."

The producers agreed that the contestants could talk to the staff in emergencies, but they should refrain from casual or friendly conversations. The camera operators broke the rules all the time, especially at night when the two contestants would mostly sit around and stare at the fire. Little jokes here and there. Comments. Pointing out creatures—mostly mule deer—with flashlights.

The cameraperson has her long hair wrapped around her head in a thick braid. She sets the camera on her shoulder and says, "Do you think I should back up?"

"Yeah, maybe twenty yards or so," says Genevieve. "I'm going to wait alongside the water. If we don't move, the fish could return."

She sits on the bank, one of the pronged spears resting in her lap. All her life, she showed a natural instinct at patience and holding still, having always excelled at hunting and fishing when she went on trips to the Boundary Waters or Canada with "the boys"—her dad, uncles, and their sons. She easily matched the prowess of her male cousins who spent countless dollars at Bass Pro Fishing Shop. Her relatives always invited her along on their annual trips to the great outdoors but never asked her on smaller excursions. No one called her to go fishing on a weekend, or to find out if she wanted to try her hand at turkey hunting. Outdoor activities, for the most part, were innate to her. Being in nature was a perfect time to meditate and clear her mind. She never thought of it as a social activity as her male family members did, or thought of herself as part of the group.

She wonders, when her relatives watch the episode, if they will feel a connection to her—the girl who they sometimes fished and hunted alongside—or if they will fixate on her nakedness. The fact that they know what their cousin or niece looks like without any underwear.

Next to the pool, her breathing slows. She doesn't move her eyes, fixating instead on the deepest part of the water where she had seen the backs of the fish earlier. She concentrates on her senses. Hearing, smelling, and the dissipating feeling of cold.

The few contestants who beat the month-long challenge are not only skilled in outdoor survival but also internally wired to push themselves past the boundaries of physical pain and exhaustion. Genevieve doesn't understand why she wants, so badly, to finish the month. It might have something to do with her male relatives and how she wishes to be perceived, but in all likelihood, she's thinking, it has more to do with this speck of herself in a galaxy of countless specks, on a wet and rocky speck of a planet. She moves sticks and stones around on this planet, lives and dies. But there is a person inside of her who she believes is her truer self, impossibly small—a speck of a speck—who she feels she could love, who is capable of surviving.

If a contestant lasts the month, they receive a few thousand dollars in prize money. She's forgotten how much it is. It's not as much as she thought it would be. Maybe it doesn't matter. Maybe none of it matters.

Minutes pass, maybe an hour. Genevieve can hear the cameraperson behind her, shifting and repositioning, switching the camera from shoulder to shoulder. On the other side of the water, a single chickadee flits between branches.

And then a fish appears. A shadow skulking along the bottom of the stream. Her stomach constricts at the sight of protein. The fish is skinny and long, and she knows it will move through the water like lightning when spooked.

Her grip tightens on the spear and she tells herself that she is going to eat today. She must.

* * *

The sun is already beginning to set—the sky taupe and pink on the edges. Daylight, in the mountains, is fleeting.

The fish on the end of her stick is puny compared to others she's caught, and its scent might attract bears, but Genevieve could not care less. Harpooning the fish had been perhaps the single greatest achievement of her life. If a bear tries to steal her catch, she will hold the fish in her mouth, take on the bear with her spear—her mighty hunting spear—and then maybe bear meat will be on the menu, as well. In the walk between stream and camp, she is naked, beaming, and unstoppable.

Her first thought is that Barry doesn't deserve any fish.

152

It is her catch, her trophy. The fat, lazy man can waste away by the fire pit, chewing like a cow on grass and weeds. But at some point in the journey to camp, practicality takes over. He is her partner. To last the entire month, they need to keep each other alive. His knowledge of plants is valuable, his extra pair of hands and feet, his companionship even. She imagines strutting into the firelight, fish held high. Barry clapping his hands and saying how the scene in front of him is almost unthinkably sexy.

When she arrives to camp, though, nothing is as expected. The sun is nearly down, and the dim light casts long shadows across the landscape. People are outlines. One of the producers—she can't tell which—and two camera people are standing over Barry, who is kneeling in the grass away from the fire, puking his guts out.

The producer is speaking through a walkie-talkie. "He just started vomiting a few minutes ago. No, no blood. It's mostly green. I don't think he's running a fever. Not shaking. Do you have chills, Barry?"

Barry spits on the ground and says, "Piss off," and then dry-heaves and gags. A spoonful of liquid seeps out of his mouth. He spits again.

The producer turns to the camera people and says, "Alright, everybody. Let's give the contestant some space." Genevieve walks over and puts a hand on Barry's shoulder. She kneels down and says, "Hey, are you okay?"

"No worries, love," he says.

"Are you sick?"

"Could be, but I don't think so."

"Do you want them to call you a doctor?"

"I'll be okay. I just ate too many dandelions."

"You did eat a lot."

Barry takes a long breath. Genevieve thinks he is about to throw up again, but he doesn't. Instead, he says, "Do you think this footage will make it into the film?"

"Probably, yes."

"This is all quite stupid, isn't it? I mean this whole thing. Wait till my mates get ahold of this. Me stark nude and speaking

Dutch in front of the cameras. My naked asshole everywhere."
He shakes his head and looks up, seeing for the first time the fish
stuck to the spear. Staring, he wipes his mouth on his forearm.

"Look what you've done," he says. "Incredible you."

She helps him to his feet, and they slowly walk away from
the cameras toward the shelter and flickering fire.

* * *

Week two contains no more fish. Genevieve ventures
to the stream daily, in hope, but the cold water is empty. Barry
finds, not far from camp, a grove of wild wax currants, and they
live off those, mostly, with a sprinkling of other plants and roots,
and, of course, boiled water or rainwater.

Barry already looks at least twenty pounds lighter. He no
longer sports a double chin, and his belly is half the size. Genevieve would guess she's down around ten pounds. Her breasts
and hips have shrunk, but her stomach seems constantly upset
and distended. The hunger is always there in the background,
gnawing away at her life force.

There is little talk anymore. They spend about two hours
each morning searching for nutrition and gathering wood. The
rest of the time they sit by the campfire, staring at the flames,
drained to empty but unable to sleep, thinking about food and
red wine and sugary candy and coolers of beer and whirlpool
bathtubs and knit quilts and king-sized beds with hills of white
sheets.

At the start of the third week, Genevieve decides to go for
a hike. She's sick of walking to the stream and finding no fish, so
she heads at an angle up the mountainside. The cameraperson
with the thick braid follows. Genevieve has started to think of
this woman as her own personal videographer.

The summit of the mountain is visible near the low
clouds, but likely at least a day's hike. She thought when she
was first transplanted into this wilderness that she would climb

154

to the top one day with her partner. That, along with so many things, seems an impossibility. If nothing else, this experience is teaching her how many things the human body can't do—how it crumbles when not surrounded by comfort and resources.

But she could always come back, she tells herself. She could return to the mountain with gear and supplies and, most importantly, clothes.

"That's a pretty stiff north wind," she says to the cameraperson.

The cameraperson nods, continuing to shuffle sideways and film the naked woman's progress up the slope. Around the corner is a small outcropping of boulders, creating a natural overlook of the valley and six or seven peaks to the south. Genevieve heads toward the boulders. It is less than a third of a mile, but she only makes it partway before completely winded and needing to rest. She covers her kneecaps with her hands and tries to catch her breath. Her head swims in dizziness.

"Genevieve," she hears the cameraperson say.

She looks up to see the woman standing right next to her. The camera is pointed down at the grass, and the woman has a pained expression on her face. In her left hand, she holds a candy bar—chocolate and peanuts. The wrapper already unwrapped. It looks fat and beautiful. Bursting with calories. Dripping with flavor and sweetness.

"Take it, sweetie," the cameraperson says. "You're starving to death."

Genevieve stares at the candy bar. She wants it so badly. "I can't," she says.

"Yes, you can. Nobody is around. You need it."

"I don't want to cheat."

The cameraperson steps closer and slips her arm behind Genevieve's back. Genevieve's head spins, knees close to buckling. She feels the woman's strong frame beside her, holding her up. Before she can understand what is happening, she tastes chocolate in her mouth. The woman is feeding her, she realizes. The woman is feeding her the candy bar, and she's chewing and swallowing and trying not to moan in pleasure or sob or laugh or scream.

* * *

From the rocky vista, Genevieve surveys the valley. It's so beautiful—breathtaking actually. She can still taste the chocolate that the cameraperson with the thick braid fed her. The guilt of peanuts on the sides of her tongue. At first, she thought her hunger so great that the candy bar wouldn't matter. A drop in the bucket of three week's starvation. But less than five minutes of digestion later, she feels returned from the dead. The cameraperson is also back to life, now, circling Genevieve, filming in panorama with the contestant in the foreground.

Does cheating matter in a place like this? Genevieve isn't sure. The show is real but fake at the same time. If this were true survival, there wouldn't be camera people and producers and medics milling behind the scenes. There wouldn't be a way to call for help if all else failed. If this were a real emergency, she and her partner would stay on the mountain for a day, maybe two to gain strength, and then they would venture back toward civilization—or at least in the most promising direction. And why on earth would they possibly be nude?

The north wind gains in intensity when she steps, barefooted, to the edge of the rock outcropping—maybe a third of the way up the side of the mountain. Her hair blows across her face. There's a cold bite to the wind. A change in pressure. A front pushing its way through the valley's treetops.

Something looks unnatural about the clouds climbing over the far range. They are white at the top, but underneath the clouds are the color of charcoal, almost black.

The cameraperson turns her lens in the direction of Genevieve's stare, and then pans back to Genevieve's face.

"We're going to have some weather," the cameraperson says.

"How bad do you think?" says Genevieve.

"No, you say it. Say, 'we're going to have some weather.'"

"We're going to have some weather," says Genevieve, looking out as the clouds continue to rise over the far-off range.

The cameraperson gives her a thumbs up.

* * *

When Genevieve returns to camp, Barry has been busy reinforcing the roof of the shelter with extra sticks and branches. Inside the wigwam, he's piled cuts of pine by the dozens, like giant, green feathers, and several thick logs they've been saving.

Her partner brims with adrenaline. "We'll be ready as soon as it starts, love," he says. "We'll cover the fire with the logs. I've done this once before and it turned out fine. No tricks about it."

Genevieve falls into rhythm with Barry, gathering dry sticks and grass. Anything that could be used as a blanket or covering. She is sweating from the brisk return hike and the exertion, but she can feel the temperature dropping in the air around her. It's like a timer ticking down toward zero. The sky blackening. Clouds sinking lower to earth.

Wetness touches her forearm as she hacks at a fallen tree with the hatchet. Another raindrop on her forehead—right between her eyes. Then her left shoulder. And then two, three drops on her stooped back.

"Alright," Barry yells. He is dragging the big logs on top of the fire. She knows exactly what he's doing and why. A pyramid of fuel for the flames but also a roof. If they're lucky, the fire will stay lit through the storm.

One of the producers is advising a cameraperson how to set a video-mount in the wigwam when it starts to rain in force. Genevieve and Barry are already inside, huddled underneath as many pine branches as possible. Thunder cracks, loud enough to rattle teeth. The crewmembers flinch.

"That was really, really close," says the cameraperson.

"Shit," the producer says. "Good enough." And then he and the cameraperson sprint back toward the production trailer, their fleeing bodies pummeled by rain. The cameraperson drapes his shirt over the video camera. The producer covers his head with his hands. Genevieve isn't sure, but she thinks she can hear them laughing over the thunder, egging each other on to go faster, get inside where it is warm and dry. She looks up at the tangle of sticks above her and wonders.

* * *

For fifteen minutes, the rain is angry, and the thunder and lightning are furious. The wind picks up, and, with it, a mass of frigid air. It is the type of storm that Genevieve used to like to watch from her apartment window back in the city, with a mug of hot tea on her lap. But it is different up here, so close to the heavens and clouds, the thunder immediately overhead.

The cameraperson with the thick braid jogs over carrying a large, black umbrella. She asks if the two contestants are doing okay, and if they need medical attention. The fire—what's left of it—smolders behind her. Genevieve stares at the coals. Please stay alive. Please. If only the cameraperson would move her umbrella. Give the fire a little break.

"I'm not supposed to tell you this," the cameraperson says, "but it looks like the hard stuff will be through in the next few minutes. Just hunker down and ride it out."

"Thanks for always watching out for us, Lori," says Barry. "But it'll take more than rain to defeat me and the mighty hunter here."

He wears a brave face, but a few minutes after the cameraperson leaves, he cocks his head to his partner and says, "It's just so damn cold, love. I can't stop shivering."

Genevieve has been trying to ignore the cold, but she can feel the chill in the core of her body. The temperature has dropped into the low fifties or upper forties, but it might as well be twenty degrees. The pine branches don't provide much warmth, even though she is buried underneath a dozen of them.

"What do you want to do?" she says.

"Well, we could throw in the towel. I think about it ten times a day. We gave it a run. Now is as good a time as any."

"I'm not quitting."

"I can't leave you out here alone."

"Yes, you can."

"You're tougher than I am, okay? You win. Fat Barry is soft and incapable. I'll tell everybody it was my idea, and that I was the one who couldn't survive."

She doesn't say anything for a while. Then she says, "You know we need to share body heat."

Barry doesn't respond.

"Did you hear me?" she says.

"Yeah, I heard."

She squirms out of her pine branches, the cool exposure causing a swift reminder of how naked she is. Moments later, she slips underneath his branches, pressing her soft stomach and cold nipples against his back, as if she were the big spoon. This is, by far, the closest she's ever been to him.

His body odor nearly overwhelms her senses, and his skin feels like refrigerated meat, but she squeezes against him, determined to suck any of the warmth he has from his body. She imagines his small penis shrinking and contracting.

After a few minutes of simply breathing, Barry says, "Well, here we fucking are."

She laughs against the back of his neck, for real this time. She can already feel it between them—a tiny morsel of warmth generated from skin to skin contact.

"I'm sorry that I stink," he says.

"We both stink."

"But I really smell. I haven't had a proper bath in weeks."

"Barry," she says. "Please stop talking about it."

They both inhale and exhale slowly as the heat builds between their bodies. After a while, the rain turns to drizzle, but the north wind continues to whip against the mountain and shelter.

He says, "Did you know that I like men, too, not just women?"

"What are you talking about?"

"Men, women, the whole spectrum, really. I like everybody, if you catch my drift. I don't tell a lot of people about it, but I thought I should let you know since we are pressed up against each other without any clothes. I'm oversharing."

"Oh," she says. She has no idea why he tells her. Surprisingly, being this close to her partner doesn't make her uncomfortable. Talking, sharing intimate details, anything. Maybe she's too cold to care. Maybe this is the person inside of her taking over and ensuring survival at all costs. Her impossibly small, truer self. The speck inside of the speck.

"I can't have kids," she says. Another lie. It reminds her of the time she told the producer of the show her parents were dead. It was one of those things that could be true, in theory. She's never gotten pregnant before—that's honest enough—but she's never had sex without being on the pill.

"Christ, I'm sorry," he says. "That must be hard."

"It's fine. I'm not sure I want children anyway."

"Me neither. But still."

There is a ruckus outside. One of the camerapersons was trying to carry a large cooler full of something—maybe beer— between the production trailer and sleeping trailer, and he has fallen in the mud. All the other camerapersons are outside with their umbrellas, filming the downed man. They are living it up and jeering about how this guy falling is going to be part of a teaser for the upcoming episode. It's Mud Mountain. It's Slippery Slope. It's Rain on the Range. This guy is going to be a star.

Genevieve can see the cameraperson who fed her the candy bar—the one Barry had called Lori—standing back by the production trailer, away from the others. One hand holds her umbrella and the other hand presses against the side of the build-

160

ing. She is ignoring the foolishness between the trailers, instead staring directly into the shelter and the two contestants huddled together underneath the blankets of pine.

Sitting up as much as she can while still keeping the majority of her skin pressed against Barry, Genevieve raises her arm. Not knowing why she does it, she gives a thumbs up to the cameraperson with the thick braid. At least someone will know they are still alive.

It could be Genevieve's imagination, but, through the mist, she thinks she can see the woman smile.

* * *

Acknowledgements

First and foremost, thank you to Tony Burnett and the wonderful folks at Kallisto Gaia Press, along with Richard Z. Santos for picking this manuscript as the winner of the Acacia Fiction Prize. Thanks for the support of Valerie, Jack, Isaac, Alexander, Scott, Becky, and Nathan. Thank you to my colleagues at Northwest Missouri State University and all my past and present co-workers at Greentower Press / *Laurel Review*. This book came to be with help from the following souls: John Gallaher, Richard Sonnenmoser, Daniel Biegelson, Jenny Yang Cropp, Bronson Lemer, Ande Davis, Jose Palacios, Aimee Parkison, Frank Montesonti, Bailey Stevens, Robert Long Foreman, James Brubaker, Diana Joseph, Roger Sheffer, Richard Robbins, Candace Black, Terry Davis, Richard Terrill, Steve Pett, and Gary Roberts.

Finally, thanks to these journals for giving homes to earlier versions of these pieces: "Common" at *South Dakota Review*, "Showdown" at *Miracle Monocle*, "White Landscaping Rocks," "Viper," and "Acai Bowl" at *BULL*, "Crab," "Paperboy," and "The Birds of Joy" at *New Flash Fiction Review*, "Fish Heart" at *Brilliant Flash Fiction*, "Bubbleheads" at *Flint Hills Review*, "Kingdom of Teeth and Scales," "Ball Pit," and "Spectacular Regular" at *Flash Boulevard*, "Impossible Naked Life" at *Chattahoochee Review*, "Human Resources" at *Storm Cellar*, "Killer Saltwater Crocodile Killer" at *River Styx*, "Plucked" at *Adirondack Review*, "Day Camp" at *I-70 Review*, "You are Not Listening" at *Crack the Spine*, "Siren" and "Red Line" at *The MacGuffin*, "Hold Your Soul" and "TIME Magazine Person of the Year" at *Big Muddy*, "Palestine Boy" at *Water-stone Review*, "The V Scale" at *Cardinal Sins*, "Liar, Liar" at *Defunkt Magazine*, and "Rubber Horsey Heads" at *MoonPark Review*.